The Virgin

WOL-VRIEY

Burning Bulb
PUBLISHING

Other Books By Wol-vriey:

The Bizarro Story of I
Meat Suitcase
Chainsaw Cop Corpse
Vegan Zombie Apocalypse
Boston Posh (Bud Malone #1)
Vegan Vampire Vaginas
Vagina Mundi
Melanie Nemesis Catchpole
Bizarro 101: A Basic Primer
Boston Corpse (Bud Malone #2)
Dr. Orgasm
Boston Lust (Bud Malone #3)
Pussy Transmission
Hell Dancer
Girls Are Not Smiling
Brainchew
Brainchew 2: Out of Their Heads
Blue Nightmares
Daria (An Erotic Nightmare)
Wet Bones
Mr. Ugly
Brutal
Evil
666
The Cleaverman
Perverse

Novellas and Short Stories By Wol-vriey

Big Trouble in Little Ass
Forever Ago Sunshine

The Virgin

WOL-VRIEY

Burning Bulb
PUBLISHING

The Virgin
By **Wol-vriey**

Burning Bulb Publishing
P.O. Box 4721
Bridgeport, WV 26330-4721
United States of America
www.BurningBulbPublishing.com

Cover designed by Wol-vriey and Gary Lee Vincent with a photo from the following artist on Pexel.com: Alexander Krivitskiy.
Author Photo: Lolade Akinsowon © 2014.

First Edition.

Paperback Edition ISBN: 978-1-948278-23-2

Printed in the United States of America

CHAPTER 1

Hailey

The preparation room had gray walls.

Hailey Osborne leaned over and touched her toes. She maintained that position for a few seconds, her legs parted, her feet two feet apart, then she straightened up again. She twisted her torso first left and then right, stretched her hands both sideways and up and down, and finally swung her arms around her body.

That done, she repeated the whole process again.

Hailey wasn't really exercising or limbering up. She was merely going through the motions before the contest began. It was easier and better to do something than to sit worrying in one of the room's leather armchairs.

Because there was a lot to worry about.

Or maybe there wasn't. *It's just a game show after all.* She tried to convince herself of this and almost succeeded.

Finally, Hailey stopped her stretches and did sit down. She looked around the room and then finally just leaned back and stared at her own reflection in the large mirror that hung on the wall behind the dressing table.

This prep room was about fifteen feet long by twelve wide, with a single steel door and no windows. It had three plush leather armchairs (one of which was a recliner), a large and well-stocked fridge, and the dresser, which was six feet wide and covered with bottles of cosmetics and perfumes/deodorants, foundations, lipsticks, eyeshadows, blushes, false eyelashes, every color of nail paint imaginable; and trays of jewelry—earrings and necklaces with pendants, armbands and wristbands, jeweled hairpins and combs and even tiaras. There were more cosmetics and jewelry inside the dresser drawers. One drawer was full of wigs and hair pieces.

Miriam Heller, the hostess/games-mistress, definitely wanted them to look (and smell) their best.

The prep room had no television. Hailey wished there'd at least been a radio or stereo system provided, or a laptop with movies and music on it. On arriving here, she'd given up all her personal belongings, including her cellphone. She sighed in frustration. A little music would have helped pass the time, helped her to relax.

But I'm prepared to wager that they don't want us relaxed: they want us all as tense and on edge as possible.

The final piece of furniture in the room was the weapons rack. Hailey had so far avoided paying too much attention to the rack. Instead, her gaze flickered from the jewelry on the dresser (a lot of it was utterly gorgeous and she was certain most were designer pieces), to the fridge (which was filled with protein bars and energy drinks), and to the digital clock on the wall beside the giant mirror (which informed her she had twenty minutes to showtime.)

Showtime. Damn. I must be crazy. I can't believe that I'm actually here and about to go through with this. What if I don't survive it? Is this actually worth the risk? Oh, hell yes, it is.

That settled for the moment, Hailey Osborne returned her gaze to the mirror and just stared at herself for a while. She stared with distrust at the 20-year-old reflected back at her. She was short but had a good figure. Long blonde hair framed her face and her eyes were a cool blue.

Hailey had been offered both a hairstylist and a beautician, but she'd turned down the offer; she was too nervous to make up her mind on how she wanted to look. But in this respect she was almost alone in her decision. Altogether there were five female contestants on the show and three of the others *had* accepted to have a beautician attend to them. Hailey, however, had wondered how anyone could be calm enough for vanity at a time like this.

The other four women were in rooms just like hers.

She resumed her self-appraisal. Central air conditioning had the prep room warm, which was necessary because of how she was dressed. All she had on was a white bikini and white sneakers, which showed off her toned body to best effect. The crotch of her G-string was decorated with the image of a bunch of cherries, a touch that Hailey found slightly demeaning.

Yes, I know the show's all about that but . . . they don't have to scream it out loud, do they?

Then she shrugged. *I guess they do. There is ten million bucks on the line.*

The thought of all that money made her smile. But then she frowned. *It isn't as if they are just going to hand it to me. I have to fight for it. Bleed for it if it comes to that.*

The one other thing she was wearing was a white digital clock. At the moment its screen was blank, but it was programmed to come on once the show began, and was meant to help her keep track of elapsed time and rest periods.

She looked at the wall clock. Twelve minutes to showtime. No chance to back out now. But she'd had no chance to quit for the past hour. Back then she had heard the steel bolt that secured the door automatically slide into place, locking her inside this prep room. If she'd wanted out before then, she could have upped and left and one of the three reserve girls would have taken her place. But she'd stayed and unless one of the other contestants had chickened out at the last minute, those three girls had all been sent home now.

A smile curled Hailey's lips. *So I guess I really do want that ten million as much as the other girls.*

She laughed, then frowned at her reflection. *And in that case I need to look my best for the show. Now what shade of lipstick would suit me? White for purity? Weird green? Creepy black? Or a slutty pink? Or maybe a floral . . . or deflowered red?*

Suddenly realizing that she had very little time to put on her game face, Hailey Osborne quickly applied some pink lipstick and blue eyeshadow to herself.

Deciding she looked good enough like this, Hailey now got up and faced the weapons rack. This hung on the room's right wall and had eight shelves filled with cutting weapons of every sort, everything from machetes and knives to cleavers and axes and spears. The rack even a fiberglass bow with a full quiver of arrows.

The one thing the weapons rack lacked was guns. Hailey couldn't shoot anyway; but seeing all these sharp objects really upset her. Seeing the knives brought home to her the fact that she was about to meet a lot of people who were interested in hurting her and in hurting each other; that the moment the show began, she would become merely a means to someone else's end, with that end being their becoming wealthy at her expense.

These folks really mean business, she thought, a cold chill settling over her as she surveyed the gleaming array of killing tools.

With the master clock running down to showtime, Hailey Osborne tried to make up her mind as to which of the weapons would fit her best: machete or cleaver or axe? Or maybe even the bow and arrows.

The rules said she could take whichever she wanted, and as many of them as she could carry. But staring at the weapons, Hailey wasn't sure if she wanted any of them. Or if she even wanted to use them on anyone.

CHAPTER 2

Teresa

Two rooms away from Hailey Osborne, Teresa Coombs stood admiring herself in her own prep room mirror. Her mirror was surrounded with light bulbs like this was some burlesque star's dressing room. The shiny lights amplified the effect on Teresa.

Oh my God, it's like a magic trick!

Teresa couldn't believe how good she looked after the beautician had worked on her.

At the moment she felt like a fairy tale princess. A 21st century Cinderella. True, the princess effect was spoiled by the fact that she was wearing just a bikini and sneakers, but still she found a lot to admire about her new self. She struck pose after pose in front of the mirror, approving of herself. She loved the way they'd styled her dark hair, and the way the man had made up her eyes and lips . . . and her lovely perfumes and earrings and . . .

Wow! I always knew I could look this damn good. All I need is some money. Well, I haven't got the money yet, but I made the final cut of five girls, so I'm more than halfway there.

Awestruck, she struck another pose, this time pushing her chest out. She was tall and the bikini top snugly cradled her breasts.

Teresa Coombs wasn't a narcissist; she'd just never, not once in her twenty years of life, had a professional beautician attend to her. She examined her perfect manicure again and then almost wept from the sudden intense desire to be rich that came over her.

Oh yes, this was a far cry from Lodi, Ohio and the trailer park where her parents lived. Teresa Coombs' family was dirt poor, in addition to which her father had mired himself in so much gambling debt that his bank was actually considering dropping him as a client.

Teresa was the last of three children; she had two older sisters. She'd been drifting along from waitressing job to waitressing job, trying to figure out what the hell she wanted to do with her life, until the day that her eldest sister Rosie had mockingly shown her a story she'd read on the internet, about some girl who'd sold her virginity for a hundred and fifty grand.

Reading that story had started Teresa thinking. A hundred and fifty thousand dollars was money she could definitely use. So then she'd done a lot of investigating and finally wound up here.

Actually, being a competitor on *The Virgin* wasn't where Teresa had set out to end up, but it promised to pay better, so she was game to play the game.

She finally grew tired of admiring herself and stared at the wall clock instead.

Ten minutes to showtime.

Teresa knew what was expected of her on *The Virgin*; and she fully intended to deliver the goods.

She grinned at the thought of what to come. *Oh, I'll deliver the damn goods alright.*

One thing in particular had attracted her to this show, and that was that she'd get a chance to legally hurt a lot of people. Coming from a family of layabouts, delinquents, truck-stop hookers and alcoholics, 20-year-old Teresa Coombs had grown up with a whole lot of repressed anger, and she was glad she was finally going to have a chance to vent some of that anger on someone; male or female, it didn't matter who'd be on the receiving end.

Anyone in my damn way had better beware. I intend to win this. She stole a quick look at the mirror. *I need that money to keep looking this good forever.* She stroked herself between the legs, her finger lingering for a moment over the bunch of cherries drawn on the front of her skimpy white bikini bottom. *No man is getting into this pussy today. I'll bet their lives on it.*

She checked the clock again. Eight minutes to go. She walked over to the weapons rack and grinned at the weapons on display. She'd already made up her mind which ones she wanted: two knives and an axe. She wished there were guns available; but she understood that that would make things too easy: if everyone had firearms then they could just shoot everyone else and the show would be over in five minutes.

The bow and arrows would also have been great for eliminating competition from a distance, but she had no archery training.

Another thing obviously lacking from the weapons rack was some kind of belt to keep one's weapons in. Teresa had already toyed with the idea of sticking the knives in the waistband of her G-string, but had realized they might cut through the skimpy fabric and then she'd be naked and at a disadvantage.

But Teresa, always a resourceful young woman, had found a workaround for this. Now she quickly took down the quiver from its peg and emptied it of its arrows. Then she cut off its strap and tied that around her waist, using four hairpins from the jewelry tray on the dresser table to secure it in place.

Great, now I've got a belt. She shoved her two preferred knives into her new belt. One knife was very long; the other very short. Both were hideously sharp, just like the small axe that she now picked up off the rack's bottom shelf.

Teresa balanced the axe in her hand, wondering what it would feel like to actually bury it in someone's flesh, and how it would feel to see their blood spurting. Chills ran through her at the thought, then she smiled. She'd not been trembling from fear, but from excitement.

Those other four girls won't know what hit them, she thought and walked over to the fridge and got herself a Red Bull.

She still had two minutes left. While sipping her drink, Teresa sat on the edge of an armchair and thought about the other four contestants for the ten million dollar prize. She'd met those women only briefly, while they were all being led to their rooms and asked if they wanted a makeup artist. That hadn't been long enough to get a proper impression of them other than noting their physical appearances. There was a black girl in the room on her right, and a girl with platinum hair on her left. The black girl and the girl in the room beyond hers on the right had both turned down the offer of a beautician. Each to her own; for her own part Teresa enjoyed looking as gorgeous as she did now.

Oh yes, I really do look lovely.

She tried to imagine what was running through the other girls' minds. Were they excited like herself, or were they afraid? She doubted it was the latter. Why the hell would you sign up for a game show on which you might get killed if you were scared of dying?

I'm not scared of dying, Teresa thought. *No, I'm not. I'm more scared of living the rest of my life as poor and hopeless as I've spent this first part of it.*

Then the buzzer sounded, and the door behind her automatically clicked open.

CHAPTER 3

Hailey

Axe in one hand, knife in the other, Hailey stepped out into the corridor. She wasn't alone. A tall man in a white suit stood in the middle of the corridor. And in addition, the four other women were emerging from the other rooms. There was a black girl on Hailey's left and a woman who looked quite elderly on her right. The black girl was holding two glittering axes. The older woman was clutching a fiberglass bow and had a quiver of arrows over her left shoulder.

"Follow me, ladies," the man in the white suit said when they were all out in the corridor. Then he turned and walked towards Hailey, so she stood where she was and fell in behind him once he'd walked past her, with the elderly-looking woman on her right doing the same once they reached her.

The man had short dark hair and his cologne smelt expensive. He led the way and the women all followed.

It's like a perfume and deodorant convention, Hailey thought in amusement as the other women's fragrances mingled in the air around her; just as she knew the two perfumes she'd used were also making an impression on the others.

She wanted to look around and see who she was up against, but the journey was too short to do so. About all she took note of during the short period they spent following the man was that the black girl on her left had short red hair and that the woman on her right was smiling weirdly. Hailey stole a quick glance at the older woman, then she quickly looked away again. The woman's smile was creepy, almost like she wasn't quite right in the head.

And then they were out of the corridors and stepping into a large room with lots of TV monitors on its walls. The monitors showed images of houses, both their interiors and exteriors. Some were homes, some were shops; at least three seemed to be small churches. All were however empty.

"This is the Control Center," their white-suited guide informed them. "Please seat yourselves in the chairs and wait for the games-mistress to come and address you. After which the show will begin."

Then he nodded to them and left.

There were exactly six chairs in the room, five of them arranged in a semicircle facing the sixth.

Now that they'd been left alone, the five women looked at each other. Then the black redhead said, "Well, let's all sit down. We're the semicircle."

They sat in the half-circle of comfortable chairs, with Hailey getting the chair at one end, and the black girl sitting in the other end chair. Each of the contestants studied the others with deep suspicion. Except for the elderly lady, who was smiling, all of their faces were as grim as death.

In such company Hailey found it impossible not to feel intimidated.

Her gaze rose up the walls and then swept left and right across them, peeking in corners and between the hardware in the room, searching for the CCTV cameras that she knew were recording them. She made out three or four of them concealed in the shadows like insects avoiding the light. She knew there must be several more. There had to be at least one video camera tracking each of them.

She figured there'd been cameras in her preparation room too, but she'd not noticed them, which meant that the huge dressing mirror had been a one-way mirror with the cameras placed behind it. Which brought an amusing thought to mind: Okay, she hadn't done so, but had any of the other girls masturbated in their prep room to relax themselves and release tension? And if they had, did Hi, Men! plan on showing it as part of the show? That would be both sleazy and creepy.

Her eyes moved above the monitors and settled on the Hi, Men! logo on the wall—a drawing of a nude female crotch with a bunch of lovely red cherries strategically positioned over the vagina and pubic hair.

That kinda sleazy is right up their alley, I'd guess.

"Hey, we may be here to fight for a prize and possibly even kill ourselves, but let's get acquainted," a platinum blonde girl with bored gray eyes finally said, waving her glittering machete at the others. "I'm

Jessica . . . Jessica Fox, from Tucson, Arizona. I'm a heiress—daddy's little girl. But don't'cha all hold that against li'l ol' me." She laughed coldly. "Happy to meet and maybe butcher you all later."

Weird as it was, that statement reduced the tension between the five women a little. But only a little.

Next the elderly lady, whose short black hair and green eyes reminded Hailey of her mother, smiled. "Annette Morrison, I'm a librarian."

"Hailey Osborne. I'm from Raynham; work at the Walmart Supercenter there."

"Rhianna Jackson," the black girl said from her end seat. "Got a lot of money; but not nearly enough yet. Oh, you ladies don't stand a chance against me."

At that statement the last girl smirked. "Nor do you, biatch. Trust me, I'm in it to win it."

"Not if you're in my way, honey," the black girl—Rhianna—said. "If you cross my path out in the game zone all you'll be winning is a free ride down to Hell." Despite having refused the offered beautician, she still looked absolutely stunning.

"What's your name?" Annette Morrison asked the girl Rhianna was glaring at. Hailey agreed that the girl looked tougher than nails or US Army boot leather. And alone of the five of them, she'd fashioned a belt into which she'd stuck two knives and an axe. That showed a level of resourcefulness that made Hailey question the wisdom of her being here at all.

"Hey, we're waiting," the black girl said. "Before I kick your ass in the game, who the 'F' are you?"

The girl shrugged and then laughed. "Teresa . . . Teresa Coombs. Grade-Z Ohio trailer trash trying to violently upgrade my station in life." She grinned coldly at the others. "So you see why I'm gonna win this contest even if it kills me to do so."

"Be careful what you wish for," Jessica Fox said, twirling her silver hair around an index finger. "I just might grant you your heart's desire."

With the introductions completed, there was silence for few moments, while everyone digested the facts about those they were up against. Hailey stared at the screens on the walls with their depictions of what seemed to be a ghost town.

"Hey, what are these damn images on these screens anyway?" she heard someone ask after a while. "Houses and alleyways, and is that a damn carpentry shed? And that looks like a shopping mall."

She looked down again. "That, trailer trash princess, is the game zone," Rhianna was replying. "It's where we try to remain pure for three hours, to keep our pussies locked as tight as chastity belts."

Then Rhianna glanced at her wrist, scowled when she realized that her white wristwatch wasn't working yet, and after looking around at the TV monitors and realizing that none of them had the time either, said, "Hey, I wonder what's keeping Mrs. Heller. We must've been sitting here for ten minutes now."

Hailey was about to ask the black girl a question, but then she saw that Annette Morrison, the elderly lady, was staring at *her* with a question in her eyes.

"Is something the matter?" she asked the woman.

Annette shrugged, the creepy smile never leaving her face. "You look like a really nice girl, Hailey. And so I'm just wondering what in the world a sweet young thing like yourself is doing getting mixed up in a crazy show like this one. You could die here, you know."

Hailey shrugged back. "Like, I need the money?"

Before Annette could question Hailey further, the silver-haired Jessica Fox asked: "Hey, do any of you know where we are?" She gestured with her machete at the four walls of monitors that surrounded them, with their shifting depictions of rooms, shops and alleyways. "Where the hell are we?"

That's a really good question, Hailey thought. Aloud she said: "I dunno, your guess is as good as mine. I was invited back to their Boston office yesterday, where the last thing I remember is drinking some wine and afterwards feeling incredibly sleepy, and then I woke up here."

"Same as me," Teresa said. "When I woke up, I first thought I'd been tricked by white slavers and was about to be auctioned off to some sleazy Arab sheik in the Middle East." She laughed nervously. "That would have really sucked, you know, 'cos it wasn't like when I left home I could tell anyone where I was really headed to, right? My folks think I'm spending the weekend with friends in Detroit."

"I was drugged too," the elderly Annette said. "I'm from Worland in Wyoming. But why do that to us?"

"It's so that we don't know where we are," Rhianna said. "Some of us might not survive the show and the only proof it ever held is right here."

Hailey shook her head. "We could still tell afterwards, and there would be an investigation if we went missing."

Jessica Fox laughed. "Really? Okay, girl, answer this question: Who did you tell that you were processing an appearance on *The Virgin?*"

Hailey mused on that. Actually, she'd not told anyone. She tried to remember if she'd mentioned it to her friend Bern when they'd gotten drunk together last weekend, but alcohol made the recollection super hazy. "Er, no one? But . . . but . . . what about correspondence? If we vanish someone can read our emails."

Annette Morrison shook her head. "Think, Hailey. If your case is like mine, other than for the first email reply I got, all of my contact with Hi, Men! has either been over the phone or in person, and I never took any documents away from their Denver office." She looked around at the others in the room. "Or did any of you have a different experience with them?"

The other women all shook their heads.

"What this means," Annette concluded, "is that if we all go missing, no one'll be able to find us. They won't even know where to start looking. Ladies, we're completely at Hi, Men's mercy on this crazy game show of theirs." She frowned for the first time since Hailey had seen her. "They can kill us all here and get away with it. They could even refuse to pay us for participating."

Rhianna laughed. "Oh no, they'll pay us alright. We win, we'll definitely get our money."

"What makes you so sure of that?" Hailey asked her.

The black redhead shrugged. "Well, if they don't pay *us*, how are they gonna put on next year's show? No matter how much you try to hide dirt like that, the rumor's gonna spread and then they'll have no takers."

Hailey didn't think Rhianna was right. *If we all go missing after the show, who's gonna be able to warn the next generation of greedy young virgins not to bite the dollar bait?*

But she didn't have a chance to point this out to her, because at that moment, the door in the wall facing their semicircle of chairs opened and people began entering the room. A lot of people.

"Well, girls, shit just got real," Rhianna Jackson said. "It's almost party time."

***

The new arrivals were of several sorts. Hailey could easily tell the 'suitors' by their nudity. That and the bird-masks they all had on.

There were ten 'suitors,' all muscular men with great bodies, and they all wore black 'plague masks,'—the kind with a long bird's beak. The suitors' only other attire were their sneakers and wristwatches (all black as opposed to the women's white), and a weird bulbous-looking codpiece. When the men got nearer, Hailey saw that their bulging codpieces looked odd because they were made not of fabric or leather, but of a fine see-thru metal mesh. Each codpiece was essentially a metal net over the man's penis, all of which were rampantly erect.

Looking at the ten straining erections, all as clearly visible as if one was looking through a screen door, Hailey felt a huge surge of horror. *Oh heck, Rhianna wasn't joking when she said shit just got real.*

The other four women were staring too. Rhianna was smiling, as was Annette Morrison (but then Annette was always smiling anyway). Teresa looked tough and determined, while Jessica Fox looked tough but worried, as if she'd never seen an erection before, which Hailey thought super odd, seeing as Jessica Fox was possibly the best looking of the five of them.

But maybe she's got issues with men, just wants to hurt some of them. Otherwise, what's she doing competing? She said herself that her family's rich.

One thing was for sure though, Hailey didn't enjoy staring at all these erections on display. Ten stiff and throbbing manhoods which would shortly be seeking to . . . she couldn't even think the horrible words. Oh, it had been great in theory, but now that she could see exactly what she was up against—all these straining muscles and rampant penises on display—she again wondered if she was crazy for signing the contract form.

The ten 'suitors' had arranged themselves behind the single unoccupied chair in the room, which meant they stood directly facing the five virgins. For a while, unable to help herself, Hailey stared from one male crotch to the next, then looked up at the bird mask that obscured each man's face.

Well, if they meant to intimidate me with this display, they've more than succeeded. How the hell am I going to . . .

But she found it impossible to keep her worries straight as more and more people streamed into the room and took up places around it. She was relieved to finally be able to tear her gaze from the men who would shortly be trying to deflower her and to stare at something else.

The men and women now entering the Control Center were obviously game security. They all wore dark blue jumpsuits and 'full face' black motorbike helmets that rendered their faces completely invisible. Red boots and gloves. All wore tasers at their hips and several also had guns holstered. Hailey estimated about forty security guards in here now.

When one of the women turned to face the door, Hailey read the words 'HYMEN PROTECTION' printed in bold yellow letters across the back of her jumpsuit, which she thought was a great joke.

"What're the guns for?" Annette whispered as more and more of these men and women entered the Control Center.

"To ensure no one breaks the rules," Rhianna replied. "They're playing for keeps here; they'll kill you if you fuck up. Hush, here comes Mrs. Heller."

Hailey turned back towards the door as Miriam Heller stepped into the room.

Miriam Heller was a tall woman, with long brunette hair done up in a ponytail and cold blue eyes. Her smile as she approached the five virgins was only slightly less creepier than Annette's. Well at least it wasn't as permanent.

Miriam wore a white blouse, a long brown leather skirt and thigh-high black boots. She entered the room like a queen. She walked like one too, taking slow measured steps as if she owned the world.

She stopped beside the ten naked men.

"Alright, you may all take five, gentlemen. Now that our contestants have seen what they're up against, I want to have a few words with them in private."

The men nodded and left in an orderly single file. Hailey was glad to see them go. Despite her knife and axe (weapons which she'd forgotten about since arriving here), she'd felt very vulnerable with all those stiff male organs so close by. She glanced at the others and saw that Jessica also looked relieved that the suitors were leaving. The other women didn't seem bothered. Teresa was cleaning her nails with the smaller of her two knives. Annette was giggling to herself; no doubt she was savoring some private joke about the various sizes of the men's swollen privates.

After dismissing the suitors, Miriam Heller next raised her voice and addressed the guards. "Alright, all of you head over to your assigned stations." She glanced down at her watch. "We've only eighteen minutes to showtime."

The guards began streaming back out of the room and Miriam Heller sat down quietly facing the five *Virgin* contestants.

When only two men with drawn handguns remained guarding the door, Miriam said, "Alright, girls, your watches will start working right . . . now!"

A beep sounded throughout the Control Center and the monitor screens simultaneously all went blank then blinked on again as white backgrounds against which '15:00' flickered in black digital numerals.'

Feeling a vibration at her wrist, Hailey glanced down at her own watch. The time on its white screen was −14:48. She looked back up at Miriam, who'd begun speaking again:

"In addition to its function of letting you know how much game time has so far elapsed, your wristwatch also enables us track you around the game zone. When any of you enter an area of the game zone, your watch automatically switches on the tracking video cameras in that area; and turns them off again when you leave there." Swiveling her chair on its castors, she turned and gestured to the screens, which, except for one which still showed the countdown time, had now all returned to displaying their previous images of houses and streets and alleyways. They watched as the cameras tracked the male and female guards who'd just departed the Control Center as they spread out across the game zone.

Hailey couldn't help but be impressed. She wondered how many cameras Hi, Men! had working here. From what she was seeing onscreen, there must be hundreds of them. And their range was uncanny. A woman stepped into a room and a camera instantly zoomed in on her head, the recorded images HD enough to show the objects reflected in her helmet's black visor. A man examined his boots and a camera tracked the motion of his fingers. In addition, several of the external shots must have been taken by flying drones. She saw men and women hurrying down below like scurrying ants.

"We see *everything* you do in the game zone," Miriam Heller said with emphasis. "Our sponsors and viewers insist on us showing them all the juicy details of what happens on the show." She laughed. "You'll be alone in the toilets of course, except you go in there with someone else."

Hailey nodded as did the others also.

Miriam Heller checked her watch and went on: "Now, I believe everything was already explained to you during your respective interviews, but you may ask any additional questions you have before we start."

"Er . . . how violent can we *actually* get?" Hailey asked.

Rhianna Jackson sniggered at the question, but Hailey ignored her. Now that the show was about to begin, she felt unprepared.

Hailey also felt very exposed. She had already realized that the games-mistress was acting as though she were performing for an invisible audience, each word and gesture of hers—even her smile and how she turned her head—measured for maximum effect on a group of unseen viewers. Which meant that Miriam was being recorded; and the same surely applied to the rest of them. Hailey once again wondered where most of the video cameras were hidden. Were they concealed behind the walls of monitor screens? Or were the screens themselves the video cameras; sort of like the webcams that were built into laptops? She wasn't bothered about the audience—it had already been explained to her that this show was being streamed live over the internet to a clique of very rich people who got off on the thrill of watching live violence. She didn't know many people were currently tuned in to watch *The Virgin* but, considering the size of the purse, she guessed they'd be a quite a lot.

Then she shook her head. *This may be just like tennis or the opera; entertainment that still exists because it's subsidized by the rich. You don't need a lot of people to keep a thing going, you just need a lot of money.*

Either way it didn't matter. What did matter to her was that she was about stepping headfirst into something that could easily turn very bloody and deadly. She looked around at her fellow competitors, all of whom were now tightly clutching their assorted knives and axes and machetes, and felt a shiver of intense fear.

Miriam hadn't yet replied her question. She seemed to be waiting for the dust of Hailey's thoughts to settle. She was frowning and tapping her left knee with her fingers. Hailey wished she say something.

Finally Miriam sighed. "I assumed my husband Aaron explained all that to you during your meetings with him."

Hailey was relieved when platinum-blonde Jessica Fox replied for her: "Yes, he did. He said we could go all the way—but what exactly does 'all the way' mean?"

"Yeah," Teresa added. "I mean, seeing all the security you've got, I don't wanna do something to someone and then get shot for doing it."

Rhianna Jackson sniggered again. Annette Morrison grinned and nodded.

Miriam nodded. "Oh, I see what you mean. Alright, I'll go over this quickly." Then, looking at no one in particular, she raised her voice and said, "Aaron, honey, have the techs switch from the live feed to a recap of last year's show while I fill the girls in on a few details."

There was a brief pause, a burst of static, and then a male voice that Hailey recognized as Aaron Heller's came over hidden speakers. "How many minutes should I add to the countdown?"

Miriam glanced at the monitor that still told the time. "Best we make it an additional five, seeing as they still all have to walk to their starting points."

"Okay, honey." The speakers went silent and then the time on the monitor screen altered from 12:02 to 17:02.

Hailey had a look at her watch. The same five minute adjustment had been made.

"Alright," Miriam Heller said. "Now let's get this all cleared up once and for all. Ladies, this show has no rules." She smiled coldly. "Everything—and I fucking mean *everything*—is permitted here. The one and only objective you girls have for the next three hours is to remain *virgins*. How you do that, well that's up to you. You've got deadly weapons, feel free to use them on the suitors"—she giggled—"and on each other, if you so choose."

"Huh?" Annette said. "On each other? I thought we were only up against the guys."

The games-mistress shrugged. "Let me put it this way: there are five of you competing tonight and the prize is ten million dollars." (This was Hailey's first intimation of the time of day—she'd lost all sense of time since being doped and transported here. She'd also assumed that the green sci-fi overhead views of the departing and spreading guards was merely a special affect, not the product of night-vision cameras.) "If you all keep your hymens intact, you'll share that money equally, win two million dollars each. If only two of you do, their share of the pot will be five million each . . . while if we've only one winner . . ." She paused and looked searchingly from face to face. "Well, do you get the point? You're not just competing against the men tonight, but against each other."

"Meaning we can maim and kill each other in the game zone or even deflower each other," Rhianna Jackson said. "The end result's still the same—the prize money gets split between the remaining intact hymens."

Hailey almost laughed at that. "We can deflower each other?"

Miriam nodded back. "Like I said, everything is permitted. Except during rest periods, of course. Once the buzzer sounds, everyone takes a fifteen minute break. Also, if you drop or lose your weapon, just pick up another. You'll find lots more in the game zone, along with many other things that can inflict harm on a human body. You're permitted to use anything and everything you find in there to protect yourself or attack someone else with."

"Okay, we got that," Teresa said, frowning. "But what if none of us survive?"

Miriam shrugged. "Well in that case each of your next of kin—whoever you named as beneficiary on your contract—will receive a million dollar inheritance from some long-forgotten uncle or aunt. This of course only applies if there are no survivors; otherwise the entirety of the prize money will be split between the winners." She checked the time on the monitor: fifteen minutes more. "Now, enough of that; back to business. Is there anything else that you either don't remember or want explained to you in more detail?"

Everyone thought for a while. Hailey figured there wasn't anything else she needed to know. She shook her head. "Nah, I think I recall all the rest."

"Alright then," Miriam Heller said after all the other women also shook their heads. "But still, I'll give you a brief refresher course. First thing you need to remember is . . ." She stopped and said loudly, "Hey, honey, you can switch back to the live feed now!"

There was a brief pause, then "Done, you're back live," came the voice from the hidden speakers in the walls.

19

Miriam nodded and then got to her feet. She stepped out of the enclosure of chairs and paced across the front of the room. "As I was saying, things to remember: First of all, the game zone is booby-trapped." She shook her head at their worried looks. "Not everywhere, mind you, but there are traps spread throughout the game zone. Some of them are merely dangerous. Others are quite deadly. Some . . . well . . . we've also put lots of dangerous creatures out there too. Only small creatures though. Large spiders, snakes, bugs, rats . . . take your pick."

The five women Miriam was speaking to might have been tough and willing to fight tooth-and-nail for the prize money, but her mention of spiders and rats had them looking like they'd puke. Hailey couldn't stand rats, and apparently, from the looks on their faces, neither could Rhianna or Annette, whose manic smile now altered to a look of intense disgust. Teresa didn't seem to mind rats though: Hailey thought she probably bred rodents in her family's trailer. Rich girl Jessica just looked confused; she didn't seem to know what a rat was. Oh, being rich must be so wonderful.

Miriam waved a hand at them. "No, no, ladies, no need to look so frightened. Most of those horrible critters are in cages. Some will be released if you stay concealed too long in a place—hiding out and not fighting at all is considered cheating. Others . . . well, you'll each have to watch where you place your feet. Or you might release them yourselves if you can locate the switches." She smiled. "Okay, so that's sorted out. Which leaves just two more—"

"Hey, what about diseases?" Jessica asked. "I mean STDs and the like. "Losers get fucked, right?"

"Or worse," Teresa giggled.

Hailey wasn't sure how important catching an STD might be. That seemed to be a concern for the future. If you survived that long.

"So yeah," Jessica went on, "I know we're doing this for a lot of money, but ten million isn't much use to me if I catch herpes or AIDS, you know."

"Everyone here is clean," Miriam replied her. "The suitors have all had the same medical examinations that you girls did. Remember those blood samples the doctors took from you all? Well, in addition to ensuring that we have enough of the right type of blood on hand in case we've an emergency and need to save any of your lives, those samples were also used to screen each of you for STDs. All of the suitors were similarly tested." She smiled coldly. "So have no fear, Miss Fox. Out in the game zone, catching an incurable disease is certain to be the least of your problems."

After stating this, Miriam stopped speaking and stepped backward. Her voice had been quite loud and Hailey remembered that they were once more back on camera and Miriam was performing for her unseen audience again.

Miriam bent over and began fiddling with the left side of her leather skirt. Hailey at first thought the skirt's hem had gotten snagged on the zip of her thigh-high boots but then Miriam straightened up again with something in her hands.

It took a moment for Hailey to recognize what the games-mistress was holding up. And then she and the others gasped. Boot and all, Miriam had just removed her left leg. Hailey would never have guessed that Miriam had been wearing a prosthesis. The artificial leg went quite a bit higher than the knee, with its straps dangling out of the top of her boot. Miriam's stump was invisible beneath her skirt.

Miriam Heller stood there on one leg and held her prosthesis out like an offering to the five virgins. "I lost my left leg while protecting my hymen, which I can assure you girls is *still* intact," she said with pride. "Now the question tonight is—how far will you go to preserve yours? Remember, all I got for my efforts was pain, but *your* prize is ten million bucks!" She raised the fake leg high, waved it around, and then bent over and began reattaching it.

"Damn, she ain't fooling around!" Teresa whispered to Hailey. "This biatch is playing for keeps."

Hailey nodded back at Teresa, not trusting herself to speak. *Huh? Her hymen's still intact? And she's married?* Hailey figured Miriam Heller had to be about thirty-five years old. *What sort of relationship does she have with her husband? Or is the guy impotent?*

She glanced at the others. Even the ever-smiling Annette looked suitably impressed.

She glanced at her wrist. Ten minutes more.

"Now you're almost ready," Miriam said, rejoining them and once more taking her seat in her chair, prosthetic leg back in place. "But before I escort you to your starting points we've just enough time to watch the conclusion of last year's contest together. It's a very short clip and one which I'm sure will give each of you a crystal clear understanding of what's expected of you tonight." Something seemed to occur to her then, because she paused and added: "You'll be leaving here together, of course, so please don't entertain any ideas of attacking each other while we're in the corridors. Reserve your violence for the show."

Everyone nodded. Miriam then called out, "Show our girls the clip, Aaron!"

"Coming right up, honey!" There was a brief pause and then all the screens on the front wall of the room, the one directly facing the semicircle of chairs the five virgins occupied, switched from showing diverse images of the game zone to portraying a single giant composite image.

Miriam Heller swiveled her chair around to face the screen also. "Now, watch and learn," she ordered.

Hailey and the others watched. The screen showed a street lit by bright streetlights. It was night and it also looked like the rain had just ended—Hailey got this impression from the puddles in the road.

The camera shifted towards the left sidewalk. A man—one of the suitors—lay there dead. He still wore his plague mask, but his mesh codpiece was gone and both his penis and his right arm seemed to have been chopped off. Both Jessica and Annette laughed at the sight.

"Shush and watch!" Miriam said. "This is *very* important."

The camera shifted again, locating the man's detached arm in a puddle of bloody water. It found his penis across the road, then panned up to show the window above it, which was dripping with blood. Then, before any of the watching virgins could comment on the obvious, namely that someone must have thrown the dead suitor's severed penis across the road so it hit the window and bounced back onto the sidewalk, the image was replaced by another.

This was of two women fighting. One black, one white with dark hair. Both were completely naked and dripping with blood from several cuts. Holding machetes out towards one another, they circled each other warily.

"Last year's last two contestants," Miriam explained. "And that dead guy was the last suitor whom they teamed up to kill. At this stage they'd won five million dollars each, but both young women were greedy and wanted all the money for themselves."

Onscreen, the black girl and the brunette circled one another warily. Then the brunette lunged in, swiping at her opponent with her machete. The black girl ducked out of the way of the swinging blade, and hacked down at the wrist that held it. There was no sound, but Hailey could almost hear the noise of the brunette's scream as her right hand separated from her wrist. She stood there, her eyes and mouth open wide in agony as her adversary grabbed her by her hair and then kicked her feet out from under her.

The brunette hit the ground hard and lay there jerking, with blood squirting from her stump. She would clearly be dead soon. But clearly 'soon' wasn't quick enough for her dusky opponent.

"Shit!" Teresa and Annette gasped at the same time as the black girl raised her machete high above her head and brought it down toward the brunette's neck, while her victim mouthed entreaties, doing her best to change her pathetic fate.

Hailey looked away. She could imagine what had happened next; try as hard as she might, she couldn't help seeing it in her mind's eye: razor-sharp steel connecting with flesh, steel penetrating flesh, living flesh separating into two dead pieces, blood spurting. She felt faint. Felt like she'd puke and fought her gag reflex down.

What the hell have I gotten myself into here?

"Huh? What the fuck?"

Spoken by several voices at once, these sounds of surprise from Hailey's co-competitors easily penetrated her worries. Their confusion sounded so complete that she just had to look back at the composite screen again.

Onscreen, the black girl had won. She held the brunette's severed head in one hand and her blood-dripping machete in the other. The camera panned down to the floor to catch the blood squirting from the dead young woman's neck, then back up again, slowly rising up the winner's mocha-colored body to her smirking face.

Hailey gasped too on seeing the winner's face.

Covered in blood and with her hair braided into cornrows, Rhianna Jackson looked a little bit different, but there was no doubt that she was the one onscreen.

Just like Teresa, Annette, and Jessica Fox were all doing, Hailey too turned to stare at Rhianna Jackson. "Huh?"

Rhianna merely smiled. The black girl seemed to expand with the onscreen revelation of her deadliness, to become larger than life. Her statuesque body appeared to glow with vitality; female flesh transmuting into an icon of violence.

"Yes," Miriam Heller explained, swiveling her chair back around again so she could look at their shocked faces, "Rhianna Jackson was our winner last year. We were so impressed by her performance that we offered her a million dollars up front to keep her virginity intact and compete again this year." She beamed. "We're delighted that she accepted our offer."

CHAPTER 4

Teresa

"So what'cha think of your chances now, trailer trash princess?"

Teresa didn't really hear Rhianna's mocking question. She stared at the composite image of the black girl holding high the dead brunette's severed head like she was some ancient barbarian queen, then looked back at Rhianna.

"Yeah, makes sense now," she said. "I'd been wondering how you knew so darn much about this contest."

"We're playing for keeps here," Rhianna retorted, clearly angered by Teresa's refusal to be cowed. "If you girls can't stand the heat, well then you know where the kitchen door is."

"Hell, ya ain't joking," Teresa spat right back. "But I do think I'll adapt okay."

She glanced back up at the bloodstained vixen on the monitor, then down again at the games-mistress and the women she was competing against. The others were understandably shocked.

The mousy girl, Hailey, looked like she was about to throw up. Her face was paler than a ghost's. She looked like she'd quit the contest right now if it were permitted. Seeing how Hailey's hands were trembling around the knife and axe she was holding, Teresa instantly wrote her off as a serious competitor. The girl wouldn't survive the show's first hour. *The little mouse will be fucked and on her way home before the first rest period.*

Then there was Jessica Fox, by her own description 'daddy's little girl.' A stunning beauty. Jessica was clearly rattled by the killing she'd just watched, but then her lips tightened into a determined frown and next, she unconsciously began flexing the fingers of her left hand around the grip of her gleaming machete. With her right hand she adjusted her breasts in her bikini top. Teresa felt a twinge of envy; Jessica had great breasts.

Well, if it's kicks and thrills Miss Debutante came here for, she'll surely get her fill. She's definitely competition and quite dangerous too, if only because she intends to return home alive to continue spending daddy's money. I doubt she's in this for the money, which makes her even more dangerous.

Her thoughts didn't bother lingering on Rhianna Jackson. The young black amazon (Teresa didn't think Rhianna was older than nineteen) had already proven how deadly she was. *She's my main competition. I've gotta make certain to watch out for her at all times.*

Which left just the librarian Annette Morrison. *And what's with her?* Annette's unwavering smile had Teresa creeped out. *That woman looks crazy; I'm sure she's been committed before. But . . . how the hell can you be as good-looking as she is and still be a virgin at her age? She has to be almost fifty— my ma's age! Except she's been chasing men away with an axe? Oh yes, she's definitely got several screws loose upstairs.*

Annette noticed Teresa watching her and blew over a kiss. "We'll dance together in Hell, darling."

Teresa quickly looked away from her. Annette was just too creepy. Teresa preferred scowling back at Rhianna.

Teresa's appraisal of the others had taken less than a minute. (It was now six-and-a-half minutes to showtime.) All that while, Miriam Heller had sat quietly, clearly leaving them to understand that this wasn't a joke they were about stepping into; that it involved real blood and guts—*their* blood and guts.

Teresa really appreciated Miriam's showing them this video. Her 'win by any means' motto had just taken an upgrade in seriousness. Now she realized there was no margin for error here; any mistake could prove deadly. She had no friends here; everyone was a foe. She looked down at her knives and axe and shivered.

Oddly though, she wasn't shivering from fright. She felt a tingly anticipation of combat, a growing desire to get the show started as quickly as possible.

She reminded herself that her adversaries weren't just these four women, that she also had ten men to survive. And survive she would.

She looked at the screen again. "Hell no. No one is ever holding up my head like that," she mumbled to herself.

Up until this moment Teresa Coombs hadn't given much credence to the idea that here on *The Virgin* show they'd actually be able to kill someone and get away with it. But the living proof of that fact was sitting right here with her. Red-haired Rhianna Jackson *had* killed someone—possibly two people actually, since Miriam said she and the decapitated brunette had initially teamed up to kill the castrated guard—and here Rhianna was a year later, as feisty as ever and ready to kill again, and apparently stinking rich to boot. (Teresa's initial impression of Rhianna was that the black girl looked like a million dollars. She'd since upgraded that to 'ten million' dollars. No, make that eleven—there was that additional million she'd been paid to remain chaste for another year and compete again.)

So, frigging yes—Hi, Men! clearly did have the ability to sweep everyone's transgressions here under the carpet.

"Your crimes will be as irretrievable as your virginity," was how Aaron Heller had put it to her. If she won, she'd leave the show the same way she arrived, with no fear of future troubles with the law. *I'll just be a whole lot richer.*

"How many people did you kill last year?" she asked Rhianna.

Rhianna shrugged. "Four, trailer trash princess. Three suitors and Melanie."

Teresa mused on that. Melanie would be the dead brunette. *So Rhianna butchered three men who wanted to penetrate her? Hmm, yeah, I really gotta watch out for her.*

"Still think your chances are good, trailer trash princess?"

Teresa decided she didn't like Rhianna Jackson.

No, Teresa Coombs wasn't the least bit racist, a trait that she'd inherited from her father. Mike Coombs might've had many faults, but discrimination based on skin color wasn't one of them. Mike's dinking buddies (and also whoring and wife-beating buddies) came in all shades of the rainbow, from Negro to Asian to Latino. All that was required to join the Mike Coombs friendship club was a good passion for Jack Daniels and Bud Light and a bad attitude towards your womenfolk.

"A true American's a drinkin' American," Mike Coombs would always say.

Which was the main reason Teresa didn't drink alcohol. She wanted no part of her father's philosophy.

So no, Teresa didn't have a racist bone in her body. She just disliked Rhianna on a deeply personal level; not the least because this young black woman currently stood in the way of her becoming someone in life.

Besides, Teresa reasoned angrily, *Rhianna already has eleven million dollars. So what the hell is she competing again for except she's a greedy biatch?*

Now she glared at the black girl. "Oh, you're about to find out how tough I am, biatch. This trailer trash princess is gonna kick your ass all the way into a Disney fairy tale. Which do you prefer: *Aladdin* or *The Lion King?*"

They might have exchanged hot words with each other, but right then a buzzer sounded.

"Five minutes to showtime, everyone," Miriam Heller said, rising to her feet. "Alright, girls, follow me to your destinies."

Carrying their assortment of deadly weapons, Teresa and the others got up and followed Miriam to the exit.

CHAPTER 5

Hymens R Us

Miriam Heller of course accepted that there were myriad ways to accidentally rupture one's hymen nowadays—insertion of tampons, riding a bicycle or a motorbike or horse, vigorous exercise, vibrators and dildos, and even masturbation with one's fingers, if one went deep.

She had no criticism of virgins who didn't have hymens. Losing one's maidenhead didn't necessarily equal losing one's virginity.

Some girls were born without hymens; others had hymens that were a disgrace to the name—flimsy bits of tissue that looked more like 'Welcome To My Vagina' signposts than practical obstructions to a manhood's progress. And some hymens were so fragile, one wondered why God had installed them in their location at all.

Like her cousin Sally's, for instance. Sally had broken her hymen at age ten while skipping rope in Miriam's back yard. On getting back inside the house, she'd found blood on her panties and that was that.

But Miriam was a businesswoman, and in her line of business a customer usually wanted proof of the genuineness of what he was purchasing. Which meant girls with their hymens still intact.

Or else just about any young woman could pass herself off as a virgin, if she lied convincingly enough. And some people could even deceive lie detector machines.

On *The Virgin* there must be no question as to the 'undefiled' state of the female contestants.

And so girls with hymens were the only sort that Miriam selected for her show. All five of this year's contestants had been medically examined and verified to be 'intact,' and pictures of their unruptured virginal tissue had been uploaded along with their other vital statistics for the audience to view and bet on.

CHAPTER 6

Hailey

All Hailey could think about as she followed the others out of the Control Center was what an awful mistake she'd made by signing up for this competition. She had no doubts on that score now. *I'm gonna get killed tonight!* The thought of her impending death almost paralyzed her. She saw no way out of her predicament.

(Like Teresa had suspected, given the chance Hailey Osborne would have begged out of the contest. After seeing Rhianna's display onscreen, she was that frightened.)

Once outside the Control Center, Miriam led them down a series of corridors.

Hailey paid little attention to where she was being taken. All this while she was desperately wishing that there wasn't a guard behind her, so that she could slip away through one of the doors they were passing. Because she'd been sitting right at the end of their semicircle of chairs, she was the last in line and if there hadn't been a guard behind her, she'd have bolted. She'd have been long gone before anyone noticed she was missing.

She however suspected that the guard behind her was there specifically for that very reason—to prevent any of them vanishing at this juncture. She even considered turning and tackling the guard, but a glance back had shown her that he had his gun drawn.

Shit, shit, shit. What am I gonna do now?

She'd been staring down at Annette's heels, her ears deaf to everyone's footsteps, with her startled mind looping the image of Rhianna holding up that other girl's severed head. Now, however, Annette stopped abruptly and Hailey almost bumped into her. She stopped herself just in time and lifted her head to see what had made Annette halt.

Up ahead Miriam had paused before a steel door.

Jessica was first in line. "This is your door," Miriam told her. "Once you step through it, it will automatically lock itself and you'll be unable to exit the game." She looked back at the others. "Ladies, your entrance points are all walled off from each other. None of you will meet up again until after at least fifty yards, so you'll have enough time to plan your game strategy. This goes for your encountering our suitors also. The nasty, horny men are out there waiting to defile you, but our rules don't let them ambush you right off. So good luck, all of you."

That said, Miriam opened the steel door and Jessica stepped through. Miriam shut the door behind her. Hailey heard the door lock itself: a whirr of gears and a loud and ominous click; a liquid gurgle that sounded like someone choking. Hailey doubted this door would open again even if it was bombed.

And then there were four, she thought glumly as they resumed walking, now stepping into a curved corridor down which she could already see the next door.

Hailey Osborne no longer cared about the prize money. Now, her sole concern was staying alive for the next three and a half hours.

As Rhianna Jackson stepped through her own steel door, Hailey rued the day that she'd first found out about Hi, Men!:

***

20-year-old Hailey Osborne was a virgin for a simple reason: she wasn't into short term relationships. Though she liked boys as much as the next young woman, Hailey also needed to know that the guy she was sleeping with actually cared about her, and wasn't merely with her because she was regularly parting her legs and granting him admittance to her body. She felt that a three-month waiting period before having sex was necessary to determine if the guy was serious or not.

Unfortunately, most of the young men she'd so far dated seemed to think that if the girl hadn't put out by the third date she was either frigid, a tease, or simply playing hard to get.

And so it had turned out that Hailey was still a virgin at age twenty (and with her hymen having somehow survived high school cheerleading and softball and other activities that could have torn it).

Her friends all pulled her leg about this but Hailey had been firm in her refusal to have sex simply because the guy was hot.

And then she'd realized that virginity had additional benefits.

You could sell it. There were rich men who'd pay to be the first one between her legs.

She didn't actually relish the prospect of paid sex with a stranger—it *was* prostitution, wasn't it?—but the lure of the money was impossible to resist. For one thing it meant she'd be able to quit her job. She worked as a sales associate at Raynham's Walmart Supercenter and was sick of the job because her immediate supervisor was a vindictive fellow who kept changing her work schedule without notifying her.

Her plan was to start a business with the money she got for selling her hymen; she imagined herself owning a shoe store.

Hailey had originally just tried to sell her virginity to the highest bidder. After comparing herself with the other young virgins she'd seen online, she'd figured she'd get at least a hundred thousand dollars for her hymen. Which would be more than enough for what she wanted to do.

But she kept getting turned down because the agencies were all overflowing with avaricious teenagers . . .

Her first choice, Cinderella Escorts, was booked solid. As was everywhere else she looked. The response to her inquiries was always the same: "Yes, you're definitely young and attractive, but . . ."

Apparently, all the escort agencies had long queues of defloration aspirants—with some precocious young brats reserving 'deflowering appointments' from ages as early as 14-years-old.

After a while of searching it looked to Hailey as if the earliest date that she'd be able to auction off her virginity would be in two years time; which was much too far off. She wanted—no, *needed*—the money right now. And also, her friends' constant ribbing had begun to erode her scruples about having a one-night stand with some handsome stud. True romance or not, Hailey was very ready to lose her virginity already.

Faced with the reality of things, she had conceded defeat. It looked like she'd be working at Walmart for the foreseeable future.

But then she stumbled across Hi, Men! Their website had had that simple logo of a woman's nude hips with three cherries draped over the crotch.

The Hi, Men! escort agency was also booked to the full with young women (and a few cute old maids) seeking to auction their hymens, but after doggedly applying anyway, Hailey received a surprise.

The email reply to her request began normally (and disappointingly) enough:

Dear Miss Osborne,

Though you definitely possesses all the qualities we at Hi, Men! are seeking in our virgins, we regret to inform you that at this time we do not have the space to add you to our long list of female applicants . . .

But then the letter's tone abruptly changed:

. . . However, if you'd be interested in a chance to win ten million dollars while possibly also retaining your virginity into the bargain, please call us on this number . . .

Was Hailey interested in winning ten million? Hell yes, she was interested. She copied the supplied telephone number into her cellphone and dialed. A man answered and two days later Hailey Osborne was on her way up to Boston to meet with Aaron and Miriam Heller.

First interview, second interview, batch of psychological and medical tests (including her donating a blood sample and fitness and vision tests), the contract signing, and then finally, she'd gotten the phone call informing her that she'd been accepted for the show and asking her to come up to Boston that Friday morning. And no, she didn't need to bring along anything except her toothbrush.

Hailey had been elated. She'd told her friends in Raynham that she was off to visit her parents in Boston, told her parents in Boston that she was off to visit friends in Maine, and then took a Uber up to Boston anyway.

And there in the Hi, Men! offices she'd drank that drugged glass of wine and now . . .

***

Teresa went through the next steel door. Then Annette. And then Hailey reached the end of the curved corridor and was face to face with her fears. The steel door beyond which . . .

"Well, here we are, dear," Miriam said nicely, then checked her watch. "Game time is in thirty seconds, so if you walk fast . . ."

She opened the door. Hailey looked through it. All she saw out there was a dark and narrow alley with a high brick wall on either side. The scanty lighting made the alley a little unsettling, but it wasn't too much out of the ordinary.

Alright, I can do this, she told herself. *I'm going to step through this door now and I'm gonna compete in a kickass way and maybe even—*

But apparently she'd spent too long prepping herself up.

"Oh, don't be such a pussy, girl," Miriam Heller said and shoved Hailey through the doorway into the game zone. "There's no lions waiting out there, just horny men."

Hailey stumbled forward onto the concrete, instantly feeling a warm summer breeze on her skin. Her motion stopped when she bumped into the left wall of the alley. For a moment she felt confused, then she looked back and saw Miriam waving at her from the rectangle of light which marked the door.

"Fight, girl!" Miriam yelled at her. "Remember what's at stake!"

The games-mistress shut the door. Standing there in the half-darkness Hailey heard it lock itself behind her.

No escape now, she realized. *Win, lose, or die—I'm in the fucking game.*

Then she realized the ironic humor in what she'd just thought and began laughing.

Gripping her knife and axe firmly, she took tentative steps towards the far end of the alley.

CHAPTER 7

Teresa

Teresa immediately realized that there was nowhere to hide in the alley that her door had opened into. It was a walk of darkness with the only light coming from the streetlight at its far end. The alley's walls were about ten feet high, clearly designed not to be scaled.

Not wanting to remain out in the open for too long, Teresa walked quickly forward towards the alley's other end. Overhead the sky was black and there was no moon. She caught a gray hint of clouds.

The alley was about fifty yards long, with its open end bisecting a street and then continuing on between two rows of buildings. Teresa walked until she was ten yards from the end of the alley, then she paused and listened. Miriam had said the rules didn't permit an ambush, but Teresa wanted to be certain of this before she left the alley.

Then she heard footsteps up ahead and froze, pressing herself against the bricks of the alley wall. It sounded like a single set of feet approaching fast.

A helmeted security guard walked across the mouth of the alleyway. The man paused in the middle of the road, glanced Teresa's way and nodded at her, then completed his crossing and vanished from view again. She listened to his footsteps recede and relaxed a little.

Alright, so there's no nasty surprises awaiting me out there.

Not that Teresa was overly worried about being jumped. She intended to give as good as she got. She wasn't about going down easy.

She walked to the mouth of the alley and paused. *Alright, now where am I?*

The street that the alley opened into was curved, and on Teresa's side of the road, was walled all around, in an unbroken continuation of the brickwork that formed the alley's walls. On the left, however, about fifty yards distant, she spotted another alley exit.

Then she saw motion at that exit and ducked back into hiding. Peeking out, she saw Annette Morrison boldly step out of the alley and cross the road, entering the complex of buildings on its other side.

Immediately Annette had crossed the road, a metal gate slid across the mouth of her alley and locked it shut.

The gate's appearance startled Teresa and made her pay closer attention to her own surroundings. Set into the angle of the wall beside her was an eight foot high metal bar, and looking down she saw that the ground had a metal gutter along which the gate would roll to slot into a recess in the opposite wall.

Which means that once I cross the road too, there's no coming back this way.

Still she paused, trying to get a good understanding of the game zone before she crossed into it.

The game zone was clearly the area across the road. Houses, shops and streets and grass and hedges and trees and only God knew what else. Pets? Looking left and right of her, Teresa easily recognized some of the exteriors she'd seen on the monitors inside the Control Center. The buildings across the road were of different sorts with one looming structure in the background that had to be the mall.

This place looks like part of a town. Like they transplanted a portion of a town out here. But where is this place?

However, she soon adjusted her impression of its size. Studying the curvature of the road, Teresa deduced that the game zone actually existed inside a circle bounded by the road. She however doubted that she and the other girls had walked far enough along the curved corridor to actually have circled the entire game zone.

She wished she had a map. Somewhere inside this sprawl of buildings across the road ten men and four other women awaited her. All with bad intents towards her virginity.

"Ah, da fuck," she growled finally, hefting her axe overhead and scowling at her unseen adversaries. She pitched down her voice in a comic imitation of her Uncle Elmer's drawl when he was drunk on moonshine. "I isn't gonna win me ten million bucks by sittin' on my ass out here. Hey, biatches, I'm a comin' ta git ya!"

That said, Teresa crossed the road briskly. Before stepping beneath the concealing shadows of the nearest front porch, she looked back.

The metal door was sliding across the alley and sealing it off.

Watching the huge metal rectangle roll into place and click shut, Teresa felt a sudden stab of panic. She felt as if the door was sealing her own fate.

Then she shrugged off her fear and smiled grimly. She was especially looking forward to tangling with dusky Rhianna Jackson.

Girl, I'm gonna show you just what this trailer trash princess can do.

***

By her own admission, Teresa Coombs *was* trailer trash. Just about everyone in her family was no use to anyone, not even to themselves—all her male relatives drank like alcohol was going to be banned the next day; and the women were only marginally better.

Sure, Teresa liked boys (she wasn't lezzie or bi), but she wasn't about spreading her legs for any of the local drunken Romeos and winding up preggered and getting the shit beat out of her thrice a week by a drunk husband like was already happening to her two older sisters, who'd merely followed in their ma's footsteps.

No, Teresa Coombs was much smarter than that. She figured this 'Virgin' reality show was her passport out of the family mess she'd been living with for the past twenty years. And heaven help anyone so stupid as to get in her way.

***

Teresa had no idea that the compulsory psych analysis test all *The Virgin* applicants had undergone had rated her as 'borderline psychotic due to myriad family and social status issues.'

The only candidate in the show with a higher rating of 'crazy' than Teresa was the premenopausal Annette Morrison, but Annette was crazy in a completely different way. Both women had easily made the final cut: in the world of *The Virgin*, mental unbalance was a currency to be treasured, as it guaranteed a stellar performance from those individuals concerned.

***

Standing outside the first house on the street, Teresa tried to work out her next move. *So what now? Do I look for a convenient place to hide and wait for someone to come along and then jump them, or should I go stalking them myself?*

Both options had advantages and disadvantages. If she entered a house and waited, someone was sure to show up sooner or later and she'd have the jump on them. But she also recalled that one of the contest's rules was that you couldn't hide for too long in any one place, five minutes being the time limit. If you exceeded that duration in one location, the games-mistress would trigger whatever booby-traps that location contained to get you moving again. And apparently some of those traps were deadly. Teresa wasn't about endangering herself through her own inaction.

On the other hand though, if she went out stalking her opponents, she'd be leaving herself open to be ambushed. But she'd have the advantage of taking the fight to the others, as well as flushing them out of hiding. She liked the idea of hunting people down. She'd never been a passive young woman, who let life come to her and took whatever it flung at her without question. No, Teresa Coombs was a positive sort, the kind of girl who took charge of each situation she found herself in.

In short, Teresa liked action.

Alright, let the hunt beg—

Her wristwatch vibrated silently against her wrist. She stared down at its screen.

Tap For Map, the screen flashed in red letters.

Surprised but pleased, Teresa tapped the white screen, which immediately switched to a color display of the game zone. She realized she'd been right. The area was circular, with the five streets that connected with the alleyways through which the contestants had entered it running straight from their points of entry (the two most outward of which formed the ends of a semicircle) to a meeting point at the top of the game zone.

So we only walked halfway around it, Teresa noted. *Which means I can easily cross the whole area on foot.*

The five basic 'top to bottom' routes were in turn crossed by five side streets, giving the whole arrangement of roads the look of a pyramid.

The phone screen went back to white. Teresa was about to tap it on again when a large gold five-pointed star appeared on the screen. *This is you*, the words that flashed under the star proclaimed, after which the words disappeared and the star shrunk, while the colored map reappeared. The miniaturized star positioned itself at the bottom of the middle route through the game zone, the one which bisected the game zone into left and right (or east and west) hemispheres.

Tap to Zoom In. Double Tap to Zoom Out. Swipe to Pan. For Help/Options, touch screen and hold.

Okay, I got this, Teresa thought, trying it out. The map didn't show where anyone else was though. But at least she knew where *she* was, and she realized it also meant that she couldn't get lost, no matter what happened in the game zone.

***

Leaving the front porch of the house, she set off up the street. The street was a single lane affair. Most of the buildings at this end were unlighted except for the bleed of streetlamp beams through their windows, but farther ahead every house had its lights on.

A short distance along she saw a giant TV monitor set into the outside wall of a house. The screen was idling, showing rainbow color bars, then switching to show the current game time: −2:54:41.

Looking down the road, Teresa saw a similar monitor; this one raised on two poles. The screens would remain idle until there was action to show. They would come on when a fight or a kill or a deflowering was in progress. The giant monitors were a way for the contestants to keep track of what was going on, which included keeping count of how many people were left in the show.

The extent and impressiveness of the setup made Teresa consider *The Virgin's* financial clout. *There's some serious money behind Miriam Heller. No doubt about it. Serious money.*

On reaching an open area that might have been a park, Teresa ducked across the road, wincing when she had to run under a streetlight to reach her destination.

Being out in the open is silly, 'cos everyone can see me then.

She stood panting in a doorway, realizing for the first time that there were no vehicles in the game zone, and also concluding that Miriam and Hi, Men! must have simply bought up some abandoned ghost town somewhere and refurbished it to suit their purposes. She'd heard there were places like that dotted across the USA, towns and villages cleaned out by disaster or poverty in the old days, places where no one lived now, and no one ventured to. Places that weren't even on government maps anymore. Places even Google Maps hadn't visited.

Thinking of Google Maps reminded her of her white wristwatch. After noting that she'd so far been in the game for ten minutes with nothing happening, she tapped on the map and saw that she was about a third of the way up the street. In theory, she should have been able to see the far end of the street from where she was, but the darkness, the streetlamps, and her own position at the side of the road prevented this. She wasn't about stepping into the road and looking, that was for sure. She'd just remembered that 'granny' Annette Morrison had a bow and arrows. And Annette had come out of the alley next to hers.

She could be heading this way now. In fact Annette could be watching me right now, fitting an arrow to her bow and . . .

She squashed the thoughts. *If I start thinking of the danger I'm in I might as well just give up, shout "Here I am, boys!" pull off my G-string and lie down and spread my legs as wide as I can. I'm glad it's warm tonight and I'm sure I look silly wearing just this bikini and walking around with two knives stuck in my makeshift belt and an axe in one hand. Alright, I look both silly and sexy and dangerous.*

Then she frowned. *But where is everyone? If I'm looking for them they oughta be looking for me too, right? So where are they? Hiding?*

Then it occurred to Teresa what she'd been doing wrong. She looked at the building beside her. *Oops, I'm just lurking outside here, when I should be knocking down doors and pulling those dirty suitors out one by one and kicking their asses. And that goes for the biatches too!*

A cold smirk settled on her face. Waving her axe like a flag, Teresa walked towards the nearest building, which had two storefronts: a drugstore and a barbershop.

She was just about to push the barbershop door open when a gut instinct—a feeling that someone was watching her—made her turn around. She'd only moved a fraction of an inch when an arrow whistled through the air and thudded into the frame of the barbershop door.

Annette? But . . . ?

For a moment Teresa stood there, too shocked to move. She'd actually felt the arrow part her hair, felt either its head or shaft run smoothly along her scalp. She flung a hand up to her head, realized she was bleeding, and then realized that Annette must be hiding across the road and shooting at her. She looked across the road, caught a flash of motion and glint of metal in a house window, and flung herself sideways.

There was a blur of flying death behind her and then the barbershop door exploded into a thousand shards of glass. But by then Teresa was up on her feet again and running, tearing down the street like a terrified fox with hunting hounds on its tail.

She heard the whistle and thud of another arrow inches from her head as she ducked into the next side street, then she kicked open the second front door on the left and leapt in through it. She shut the door behind her, switched off the lights and sat on the floor to think.

Damn that biatch Annette! she fumed. *I'm gonna kill her for this.*

It was only now that Teresa realized she'd dropped her axe and also lost the smaller of her knives during her flight.

Dammit! she thought, looking around for something to staunch the flow of blood from her head.

All across the game zone giant monitors switched on and replayed the action for all to see.

CHAPTER 8

Hailey

Hailey was slowly coming to terms with tonight's nightmare. She was hiding in a house in the middle of No. 5 Street (the main routes being numbered in sequence) and was watching Annette's aerial arrow assault on Teresa on the giant monitor suspended across the road from her.

She yelped when the first arrow hit the door jamb, and her heart seemed to leap up into her mouth when the second shattered the glass. Yes, sure it was a competition, but she felt relieved on seeing Teresa scamper away unharmed.

Her first, instinctive response to the attack had been to call the police and tell them a crazy woman was trying to kill someone. She'd scrambled about looking for her cellphone but then realized that she'd handed it over to the show's producers on her arrival here. That was when the gravity of her situation really hit her.

I'm shut away in here for the next three and a half hours!

The monitor across the road also showed an inset image of Annette, who was additionally framed in a window, and who was calmly fitting arrow after arrow to her bow and letting them fly at her human target. The look on Annette's face chilled Hailey. There was something in the elderly librarian's eyes that was beyond sadism, beyond mere delight. She seemed enraptured, as if she was living out her ultimate fantasy.

Once Teresa safely turned the corner, the inset image of Annette enlarged to fill the screen. Annette was scowling, clearly angered at not hitting Teresa.

"Damn, I missed her," she silently spat, and the monitor blinked out again.

That left Hailey alone with her thoughts. She stepped back from the door she'd been peeking out of and shut it quietly. No telling who was watching out there.

There's nothing else for it, she thought, shaking her head at the knife and axe tightly gripped in her own hands. *I'll just have to live the next few hours of my life by Miriam Heller's rules. I honestly don't want to kill anyone, but if I don't they're going to kill me instead. They're all crazy, and I must've been crazy too to have signed up for this!*

Of course there was the desperation option of simply walking out into the street and yelling "Here I am, boys—come and get me!" at the top of her voice until one (or more) of the male suitors found her. Then all she had to do to quit the contest was lie down (or get on her hands and knees) and spread her legs (or buttocks) wide enough to grant him (or them) easy access to her secret garden.

He enters my orchard and plucks my cherry and I'm free to go home . . . alive. I'll just be a little sore between the legs . . . and I'll also be as broke as I was before coming here. So thanks, worries, but no thanks. I'm going through with this. I want that prize money as much as the other girls do. Hey, me, that's a great idea— whenever you feel like quitting the show, just think of the money instead!

That decided, Hailey had another look around the house she was standing in. Actually 'house' was a misnomer for her current location. Though seeming normal enough from the outside, the interior of this clapboard building reminded Hailey of a shed or a barn, the space she stood in being merely one huge expanse with wooden beams and pillars holding the roof in place. There were no true rooms, just wooden partitions dividing the space, and no doors in the openings connecting the different areas either. Nor was there a ceiling overhead. Except for a trestle table in this front room with a few nails on it (which a carpenter had clearly left behind), there was no furniture of any kind in the building either.

This house is a framework, like the kind they build for movie sets to create the illusion of a town. But the first house I entered was real, though it smelt really old. This one's like a fake-front building? It must have been built just for this TV show.

She could see clearly enough in here. She'd chosen and entered this particular house because it stood right beside a streetlight, which meant that she didn't need to turn on the house lights to have a look around. All the buildings apparently had electricity, but turning on any lights in here would be tantamount to giving her position away.

She glanced down at her left wrist. Her white game-watch had a flashlight (selected via Options). She turned it on and a thin beam of light projected forward over her middle finger, so all she had to do to see things was point her left hand in their direction. She was certain that with the bright glare of the streetlight outside the house, no one would notice this little light beam inside.

She aimed the light upward, wanting a quick look at the space beneath the roof. She had an intuition that there were things hidden up there that she might not like if she encountered them.

At first everything looked normal enough. Electrical wiring was tacked to the overhead beams, with an electric bulb dangling halfway along its length. The wire continued along the beam and vanished somewhere beyond the plywood partition which created a front room for the house, after first trailing a cable down to feed a wall socket. Hailey moved the thin beam back again. She was certain she'd noticed something up there. The streetlight's glare entered the windows in a thick beam, which, though it illuminated the house well enough, also created shadows overhead. It was these shadows that Hailey was suddenly desperate to investigate.

Finally, however, Hailey found what she was looking for. A small metal cage sat concealed amidst the rear rafters, and if her eyes weren't deceiving her, there was something moving inside the cage. She couldn't tell what that something was—rats or a snake or whatever—but once her flashlight beam hit it, it swarmed about (or writhed) within its confined space, making quite a racket. She shivered as she watched the thing move inside its prison and then shifted the light off of it. Instead, she tracked the thin cord that ran from the cage. The cord ran down one of the support pillars and vanished somewhere in the back of the house.

Keeping note of which support pillar it was attached to, Hailey walked around the partition for a look. She held her knife out in front of her in case of any unpleasant surprises.

There was less illumination on the other side of the partition. She shone her light over the room's contents. The place was piled high with cartons. She quickly opened a few. Most were empty, but one had a few rolls of duct tape in it. She moved away from that carton and stepped deeper into the room, once more shining her light upwards. She quickly located the cord that came from the cage in the rafters, the living content of which had once again gone silent.

Keeping silent herself, Hailey patiently traced the cord down the wooden support pillar to where it vanished amongst some piled cartons. She was about stepping forward to pull those cartons away, when on a whim she shone the flashlight down at the floor instead.

She gasped. About a yard ahead, the cord she was tracing lay directly in her path, suspended six inches above the wooden floor, and with both of its ends invisible because of the cardboard boxes on both sides.

It's a tripwire, she realized. *If I'd taken three steps more, I'd have kicked it*—she looked up, realizing also that those three steps would have brought her directly under the overhead cage—*and kicking it would have dropped the cage's contents right on my head.*

Shuddering from the thought of something scaly or furry falling on her mostly naked body, Hailey quickly backed out of the room again.

She tapped on her wrist map, zoomed in and scowled. She examined the map critically, wishing she could simply reach one of the blue dots. The blue dots where chapels. There were four of these and they were places where you were safe for fifteen minutes. No one else could enter a chapel until you left it, so there was no chance of any harm coming to you inside one of them. But you couldn't enter the same chapel twice in a row.

In theory one could simply dash from chapel to chapel throughout the contest and stay safe. But of course the practice was much more complex. The chapels were situated at strategic locations, so to reach them one had to run a gauntlet of dangers which made the risk not worth the effort.

Most important, none of the four chapels was near her right now.

After taking a few moments to firm her resolve, Hailey opened the front door and slipped out of the frame house.

***

The houses up ahead had their lights on, so Hailey crossed the road so she could remain in the darkness. Barely a minute later, she heard voices—the first human sounds she'd heard since entering the game zone. She wasn't near any doorways so she hid behind a tree.

She'd just concealed herself when two suitors walked out from the side street up ahead.

"Where the heck are all these prudes?" one man asked the other. "You'd think they were hiding from us."

The other man laughed. "Hey, virgins! We've got something hard for you!"

The pair walked past Hailey's place of concealment and she got a good look at them. Both were tall and well-muscled, with well-defined six-packs. Their faces were of course concealed by their plague masks. Hailey admitted that the black bird masks the suitors wore were a touch of creepy genius—the masks completely dehumanized the men—looking at them she felt more like she was staring at two demons who intended to ravish her body, than at flesh and blood.

And then of course, most prominent of all were those bulging codpieces the suitors wore, with its mesh so sheer that she could see both men's stiff penises throbbing within them. The effect was similar to that of wearing a negligee of the flimsiest silk—being naked while actually being dressed.

Hailey watched the men walk past, the sight of their bare buttocks and muscular backs stirring a faint shimmer of lust in her. Both men carried gleaming machetes and one of them was also holding a roll of duct tape.

Shit! she thought. *I should've taken some duct tape too! Be great to restrain someone with if I need to!*

But she wasn't going back across the street to get some. Maybe she would find some in the next house she entered.

The two suitors crossed the road and entered the house right next to the one Hailey had just left.

Okay, time to get the hell out of here!

However, as she was about stepping out of hiding, a muscular arm slipped around her neck.

"Hi, hon," a deep male voice said. "How 'bout if you and me have some fun?"

Hailey groaned. *How the hell didn't I hear him sneaking up behind me?*

She mentally answered her own question: *It's because you were too focused on those other two, you dumbass! And now look what's happened! You're about to go home early.*

She was pressed up against the suitor's muscular chest. It felt warm and snug against her, and she almost felt like giving in. But then she remembered the money she'd lose if she quit.

"Now, just put down your weapons," the man said. "Then we'll get down to business right here."

He was still behind her, still had his arm around her neck and couldn't see what she was doing. She dropped the axe.

"Drop the damn knife too, girl, except you want me to get rough with you. I'm about to pop your cherry anyway, but I'll go easy on it if you don't make a nuisance of yourself. Otherwise I'll tear it to shreds like a freight train splattering a wino who stepped onto the tracks." For emphasis, he squeezed one of her bikinied breasts and then the other, and after this his hand moved lower, snaking down her midriff and under the top of her G-string. His probing fingers made her tingle with both excitement and revulsion.

"I'll do what you want. Just go easy on me," Hailey said as if she meant to do as he'd ordered.

Then, surprising herself with her own speed and determination, she rammed her knife backward at the suitor's leg. She felt the steel connect with flesh and penetrate it and felt the spurt of warm blood over her fingers. The man howled in pain and Hailey pushed the knife in further.

By now, he'd let go of her throat and so she could turn around and see where she'd stabbed him. The knife was buried deep in the outer fleshy part of his right thigh, blood was spurting around it, and he was holding his leg and grunting in pain.

The suitor was making no attempt to remove the knife and so neither did Hailey. Best she leave it stuck where it was hurting him.

But he was still trying to grab her, his free hand reaching for her.

She looked at his face, realized that she couldn't see his facial expression because of his bird mask, and then stepped in close and kneed him in the crotch instead. The way his penis was throbbing in its mesh codpiece was angering her.

So you wanted to stick that inside me huh? Well, here's my thanks, Hank!

However, Hailey instantly discovered her mistake. The codpiece might have looked as flimsy as lace, but in reality it was as strong as steel. All she got for kneeing him was a sore knee.

She stepped back, picked up her axe from the ground and then turned and ran off. She realized she needed to get away before the suitor's moans of pain alerted someone else.

***

After running for about a minute Hailey entered another dark house. She needed to use the toilet; fright had her wanting to pee.

Once she'd emptied her bladder, she rinsed as much of the suitor's blood as she could off of her body, then she returned to the living room and sat in an old armchair. This house was a proper building, though its interior was largely unfurnished. It was also very old, making Hailey wonder for a moment if the contest was being held in some out-of-the-way ghost town; somewhere long abandoned and forgotten.

Here there were no streetlights outside and she sat in the darkness, though fully aware that for this house to be part of the game zone it was certain to be outfitted with hidden CCTV cameras which were recording her every action, possibly even the changing expression on her face.

She looked at her watch, which in this dark space had now automatically reversed its display to white letters on a black background. Depending on user choice the wristwatch could either show 'time elapsed' or 'time remaining' and she'd set it to show 'time elapsed.' (Hailey was trying to be optimistic here and view the philosophical glass as 'half-full' rather than 'half-empty.' She knew from past experience that she'd quickly fall into a panic if she kept being reminded of how much time still remained for the show to end.)

What was it that Miriam said again? Our watches are used to track us through the game zone, turning the cameras on and off?

Then she forgot about the show's video wizardry and turned her contemplation inward, her eyes fixing on her bloodstained G-string.

I stabbed that man. I stabbed someone! I actually stabbed him!

She was trembling from the emotion of her action. She'd never intentionally hurt anyone in her life, and was surprised that she— who'd imagined she'd wither under the first assault she encountered— had reacted so violently and had done so without hesitation of any kind. She'd experienced no moment of doubt between thought and action, she'd just realized what needed to be done to free herself of the suitor and then done it.

She regretted stabbing the man, but . . . *Well, what else was I supposed to do? I don't want to go home empty-handed!*

She sighed. *I don't have the time now to worry about the rightness or wrongness of my actions. What is important now are the consequences of those actions: do they get me where I need to go? Do they keep me alive and 'intact' for the next*—she checked her watch again—*two and a half hours?*

For the first time, Hailey began thinking she had a chance in the competition. *So long as I steer clear of Rhianna Jackson, of course.* She wondered how the black girl was getting along; if she'd killed anyone yet.

Hailey wasn't near a monitor, but she knew the screens would have replayed her fight with the suitor. *And Hi, Men's online clients will be delighted and the betting will grow more fervent and with one suitor hopefully disabled, I'm that much closer to winning and . . . Screw that! I have to keep my mind focused. The question now is, what do I do now?*

She'd noticed a few boxes in one of the rear bedrooms, so she turned on her watch-light and left the living room to search for an additional weapon or maybe some duct tape.

She found no duct tape and returned to the living room feeling frustrated. She was caught in the grip of unfamiliar emotions. Unknown to Hailey, her first taste of violence had whetted her appetite for more. She was impatient to get on the hunt for some of the others, to make her own mark on *The Virgin* show.

She paced back and forth across the living room. *No, I'm not going to be a scared rabbit, sitting on my ass in here and doing nothing, and—*

Hailey was so caught up in her own thoughts that she at first ignored the quiet click that sounded somewhere in the room; somewhere close by. And even when her thoughts caught up with her ears, she at first thought she'd merely heard the wind rattling a windowpane.

But then, she remembered the cage she'd noticed up in the rafters of the first house she'd entered. And now she imagined she could hear a rustling noise and more rattling. And the noise was coming from somewhere inside this living room.

Oops. She realized what had happened. She had no idea how long she'd been hiding in here, but it must've been too long by the show's rules. So they'd triggered something to flush her out of hiding.

She felt the need to see what they'd sicced on her. By now she'd determined that the noises were coming from the old armchair she'd earlier been sitting on.

Now the creature's trademark noise was unmistakable. It sounded like a baby was shaking a giant rattle in there; or an orchestra of tambourines and maracas.

Hastily grabbing her ax from the windowsill, Hailey crossed to the front door. There, from a safe distance of about ten feet, she shone her watch-light on the armchair and stood watching it.

She trembled with shock and fear when the top half of the chair's backrest popped open and the thick body of a diamondback rattlesnake emerged from a recess built into the armchair. The trap's door creaked as the snake slithered down over it and plopped onto the seat of the armchair.

The rattlesnake noticed Hailey and its rattling increased. It hissed at her. Hailey suspected that the reptile had had its poison glands removed and was here merely to scare any wayward contestants, but she didn't intend to hang around to find out for sure. She couldn't imagine what would have happened if she'd still been sitting in the chair, lost in her thoughts of glory, when it had emerged. She would utterly have died of fright. And even if the snake wasn't deadly now, it could still bite; and she disliked snakes anyway. Just seeing this one made her want to pee again.

The rattlesnake dropped to the floor and began slithering towards her. Without taking her eyes off of it, she reached behind herself and slowly opened the front door. Then she stepped backwards out of the house. In the nick of time she remembered that there were steps out there, and so didn't fall and hurt herself.

Once safely outside, Hailey quickly forgot the rattlesnake. Her mind filled up again with images of herself hunting down the other contestants and suitors. She turned her watch-light off and then, without bothering to find out her location from the watch's map, she set off up the road.

CHAPTER 9

Miriam

Cunnilingus always relaxed Miriam Heller. Having her vagina licked was magical, and then . . . that sweet release, which always felt like she was being bathed in honey.

Unfortunately, at the moment her husband Aaron was busy with the technicians. Miriam could have done with him kneeling between her legs and getting busy down there. Sex would have reduced her anticipation and killed the boredom of waiting for the contest to switch into high gear.

Miriam sat alone in her Control Center, watching the screens ahead of her. The images on the room's myriad screens flowed like water, with the software program that oversaw the CCTV cameras pulling the most relevant images to the center screens, so that rather than the watcher having to go to the action, it instead came to her.

With over a thousand video cameras out there in the game zone, this was the best way to handle the live feeds.

Little had so far happened. But it was like this every year. Things started off slow and then built up exponentially. This first hour might not see any casualties, but just wait till the middle or final hour and the show would degenerate into an all-out free-for-all. This stage of the competition was much like the early rounds of a boxing match, when the fighters danced harmlessly around each other before one finally knocked the other out.

Now everyone was still being cautious and hiding, everyone keeping to the roadsides. Very soon the girls and guys would all grow bolder and start *penetrating* (she shivered in mingled fear and delight as she thought that terrible word) the spaces between the buildings, but for now almost all of the onscreen activity was concentrated alongside the roads.

She'd been pleasantly surprised by Hailey's escape.

Here on *The Virgin*, the pay scale was much like that in porn, which was where Miriam had gotten the idea in the first place. Because they were the real attraction, women in porn made four times as much money as their male costars did. Here, however, the disparity in pay was even higher. The only reason anyone watched *The Virgin* was to see the virgins, so the girls earned the lioness's share of the money.

For their part, the ten suitors shared a fixed purse of a million dollars flat. This was guaranteed and the sum would be split between the survivors. Last year, there had been no male survivors and Hi, Men! had kept the money. This year would hopefully be different, as having winners of both sexes helped future recruitment drives. The suitors also got a $200,000 bonus (divisible between participants) for every defloration they were actively involved in.

Just as with the ladies though, there were no rules concerning the male competitors too. They could form alliances or backstab each other to their heart's content. Miriam giggled. They could even fuck each other if they liked. This was adult entertainment after all. Money and ratings were what show business was all about. The bets were already astronomical and the money continued to pour in.

From its humble beginnings four years ago, *The Virgin* was now an underground phenomenon.

At least four African presidents and three Eastern European ones were currently logged in and enjoying the show via Hi, Men's ultra-secure web app, which offered the latest in end-to-end encryption, and which, determining viewer identity via webcam, would shut down and lock the viewing device if an 'unsafe' person tried watching the show.

So, as she stared at the screen and wished her husband was here giving her head to pass the time before things really picked up, Miriam Heller didn't really have much to complain about. Well, except her missing leg. It was very annoying being incomplete, even if you had lots of money.

***

One autumn night fifteen years ago, 16-year-old Miriam Oates had accompanied her 18-year-old neighbor Johnny Smith out for a night of fun.

Miriam's widowed socialite mother Janice wasn't home at the time and even if she had been, the woman didn't approve of Johnny anyway. Miriam's family had money, Johnny's didn't, and that was enough reason to ostracize the kid.

Anyway, Miriam sneaking out of the house with Johnny was merely a stage in her teenage rebellion, asserting herself against the 'tyranny of parental rule' as she put it.

The problem was that she and Johnny had different ideas about the state of their relationship. Johnny saw her as his girlfriend and felt they were ripe to have sex. Miriam, on the other hand, merely viewed Johnny as someone to have fun with, and also as a great way to anger her mother. She definitely didn't think of him as her boyfriend, and most definitely didn't intend going all the way with him.

Okay, so she had given him a handjob or two when he'd gotten too randy with her, but that was all.

So . . . well, that night they drove out of Oakland, New Jersey to a quiet place in the woods. Johnny got out a case of beer and they sat drinking, and after a while one thing led to another and they began kissing and petting in the backseat.

Now, normally when they got to this point, young Miriam Oates had always cooled Johnny off with a handjob, which he'd been really appreciative of (though in retrospect this did reinforce the 'boyfriend/girlfriend' image in Johnny's mind).

Tonight, however, after Miriam freed Johnny's erection from his pants, he swatted her hand away, and next waved a strip of condoms at her.

"Nah, babe," he grinned at her. "I think it's time we went all the way."

"No!" she instantly yelped. In addition to the fact that she didn't want him inside her at all, the strip of condoms in Johnny's hand gave her the impression that he intended to do it more than once.

"No!" she yelped again. "No, I've never done this before!"

"C'mon, babe—there's always a first time."

"No, no—keep that dick away from me!"

Long story short, Johnny got insistent and Miriam got loudly resistant. The woods were quiet with everyone at home because the weather was cold and so no one happened by to break things up.

Finally, Johnny got the weeping Miriam's panties off. He was just about sticking his member into her center when Miriam stabbed him in the left eye with her house key. Johnny's eye burst like a tomato and he began screaming himself. While he clutched at his face and tried to extract the key, Miriam scrambled out of the backseat, grabbed her handbag and ran off into the woods.

So far, so good. Except that in her fright and relief the young virgin made a wrong turn, tripped over some exposed tree roots and tumbled down into the hole left by the tree when it had fallen over. The fall both knocked Miriam out and broke her left leg at the thigh. More damningly, the angle at which Miriam fell wrenched the broken portion of her leg in almost a complete circle.

Miriam wound up hanging upside down in the pit, with half of her left femur poking bloodily out of her thigh. The falling autumn leaves from nearby trees soon covered Miriam over.

Johnny on the other hand, had driven straight to the ER. Miriam had done a complete number on his left eye with the key. He lost the eye for good.

The thing though, is that Johnny had no idea that Miriam hadn't gone home. And he was so mad at her for blinding him that he didn't bother calling to find out if she had.

Miriam wasn't found for two days.

When Mrs. Oates finally returned from her weekend round of parties and realized that her daughter was actually missing and began looking for her, one-eyed Johnny told her what had happened.

There was a search made in the woods and Miriam was found and rushed to hospital.

She was weak and dehydrated but would survive. Her left leg had however had it: the part below the broken bone had gotten so twisted that its blood supply had been cut off and gangrene had set in.

And so Miriam's left leg was amputated.

Miriam was inconsolable for the month she spent in hospital.

Miriam's mother was infuriated with Johnny, which led to her making a phone call to a friend of her late husband's named Marko Velli, a gentleman who just happened to be Boston's most dangerous mobster. Marko was also Miriam's godfather.

A month later, Johnny Smith vanished. That same weekend, Miriam and her mother also left town, claiming they were taking a trip down to Florida to help the traumatized young Miriam forget her troubles.

Johnny had vanished because he'd been kidnapped by Uncle Marko's goons. (Actually he'd been kidnapped by a man and a woman named Lonnie Black and Carrie White respectively, the mention of their names being important because Lonnie 'Black' was actually Caucasian while Carrie 'White' was a Negress.)

When Johnny revived after being kidnapped, he was trussed up with hemp ropes, and lying in shallow water. The next thing he noticed (in addition to totally screwing up his sense of depth perception, having one eye also meant Johnny now had to turn his head to see what was on his left side) was the pair of giant alligators separated from him by a metal grille. The gators were staring hungrily at him and swimming back and forth in the water and trying to climb over the grille.

The final thing Johnny noticed was that he was lying in the water at the shallow end of someone's swimming pool and that there were three people standing on the edge of the pool and staring down at him: Janice Oates, Carrie White and Lonnie Black. Yes, and (one mustn't forget) angry young Miriam, who was sitting in her brand new shiny pink wheelchair and staring knives at bound one-eyed Johnny.

Carrie White had a Sony camcorder pressed to her face.

Johnny quickly worked out what was happening when Lonnie Black began cranking a lever that inch by inch raised the metal grille that separated Johnny from the two giant alligators. The reptiles had clearly never been lectured on the importance of patience. Even before the grille had lifted enough to permit them access, they were thrashing madly, pawing at the bottom of the pool and trying to force their head into the gap.

"NO, YOU CAN'T DO THIS TO ME!" Johnny yelled.

None of those watching bothered to reply him. Instead Miriam gave him the finger. A butler appeared and handed Mrs. Oates a glass of brandy. Lonnie Black continued cranking the lever. The grille kept lifting. Carrie While kept recording proceedings on her camcorder.

"NOOOOOOOOO!" Johnny screamed, pissing himself from sheer terror as the grille finally lifted high enough to let the alligators through.

"For God's sake, go to Hell quietly, you little rapist jerk," Mrs. Oates growled at Johnny as the foremost of the gators bit his left foot off. Then she accepted another stiff drink from the butler.

And that was it for young Johnny Smith. By the time the two giant alligators got done with him, there was nothing left of him. And since crocodiles and gators have digestive juices strong enough to dissolve nails, one must be certain too that there wasn't any evidence left either.

The motto of this story being that, guys, if the lady says no, it's generally best to keep your dick in your pants, go home, watch some porn and jack off.

***

Contrary to what all the contestants thought, *The Virgin* game show wasn't being held in some far-off and otherwise forgotten place. They weren't out in eastern Montana aka The Big Empty, for instance, where you'd not see anyone for a hundred miles.

No, the show was actually being filmed in Hailey Osborne's hometown of Raynham, MA., where Aaron Heller had acquired the lease to an old and abandoned industrial complex on the outskirts of town that belonged to one of his father's friends. They were using the old staff housing estate for filming. They'd walled a third of the estate off for privacy, then built in the 'fake' houses to give the place an external semblance of normalcy. After the show, the surviving contests would be doped again and shipped back to their hometowns, with none of them the wiser as to where they'd actually been taken.

There was an added bonus to filming in Raynham: once the show was over, the corpses could easily be disposed of—they'd be ground up and fed to the pigs on old Ed McKinney's farm, old Ed being the father of Raynham Chief of Police Tina Kravitz, an honest and upright woman who had not the slightest idea that such atrocities were being perpetuated in her legal jurisdiction.

***

Miriam brightened up considerably when the monitors focused on Annette. Annette was retrieving the arrow stuck in the barbershop frame.

"Go, girl, go!" Miriam cheered when the 43-year-old librarian stepped inside the barbershop to pick up the second arrow.

Annette Morrison's stated reason for entering *The Virgin* was simple: "To earn enough money to retire." Her reason for still being a virgin so late in life was also simple: "I've simply never met the right man."

Miriam considered the older woman as she stood framed in the shattered door. Annette was squinting; naturally shortsighted, for the show they'd replaced her horn-rimmed 'librarian' glasses with contact lenses.

Miriam had initially thought Annette too old for *The Virgin*. In her opinion, a middle-aged woman would be unable to complete against the much younger virgins. It might have been different if she'd been an athletic sort, but by her own admission, the most of a workout that Annette Morrison had ever had was standing on tiptoes to replace returned books on high shelves when there was no stepladder nearby.

Miriam's reservations had however vanished the moment she'd read Annette's psychological profile . . . particularly the part where Annette said her favorite author of all time was Drake Melville . . .

Drake Melville was from Dayton, Ohio. Three years ago he'd published a novel—*The Bleeding Oysters*—the content of which made the entirety of the Marquis de Sade's work look like kindergarten reading by comparison. The book's publication had triggered widespread public outrage that any publisher would dare put out such an 'abomination of so-called literature,' the entirety of Drake's thousand-page novel being devoted to things like necrophilia and necromancy, cannibalism, different sorts of child torture and abuse and the summoning of Satan through sex with reptiles and fish.

The book's very title itself was said to come from a practice by an ancient Scandinavian sorcerer named Ola Mimi, whose favorite breakfast was the raw testicles of young boys. Mimi ate these testicles sliced in two, hence the 'bleeding oysters' description.

Drake Melville's book was a smash hit. Miriam had read parts of it and felt the criticism was well-earned. She doubted that any sane mind could come up with even a quarter of the atrocities perpetuated by the book's lead character, a fellow named Seer Jonah, whose entire philosophy of life (and death) was one of causing agony, mutilation and misery to others, not for his own pleasure, mind you, but from the sincere belief that his doing so would bring his victims to God's notice and secure them His pity and mercy, and by so doing would gain them admittance into whichever heaven they believed in.

Twice while reading *The Bleeding Oysters* Miriam had run to the toilet to throw up her lunch. She'd quit the book halfway; some things were better left unread.

And there was more to the tale of Drake Melville. At the height of his popularity, Drake had suddenly vanished. The only clue to his disappearance was the cryptic handwritten note he had sent his attorney, in which he wrote that he had 'left town' to continue his research and to begin work on his magnum opus, *The Book of Atrocities*, which he promised would be even more shocking that his publishing debut.

Drake Melville had been missing for the past two years. His attorney received a text message from him every four months or so, claiming his research and work on the new book were both coming along great, but even AT&T couldn't work out where their famous missing subscriber was sending his texts from.

How all this concerned Annette Morrison was that Miriam had never met another person who professed to actually liking Drake's novel *The Bleeding Oysters*. Annette was the only one, and that simple fact had instantly branded her as someone special—someone to watch out for. A woman with untapped depths, both of depravity and cruelty.

Miriam smiled as Annette strode to retrieve her third arrow. *The librarian's true nature is beginning to reveal itself. The only question now is, how far will she go tonight?*

During her *Virgin* interview, Annette had revealed that her two hobbies were archery and sewing—she liked making her own clothes.

Miriam was already very impressed with Annette's archery performance. She however doubted that being a seamstress would do the woman any good tonight.

CHAPTER 10

Teresa

Teresa's scalp stopped bleeding while she was searching for something to staunch the blood flow. She was relieved; the path of the arrow's flight meant that blood from the wound had been running down into her left eye. She patted the matted patch of hair on her head and swore revenge against Annette.

I'm gonna get her tonight if it's the only thing I accomplish here!

Then she took proper notice of the house she'd taken refuge in. Her eyes roved up and down the rough wooden walls, the bared rafters overhead, and the lack of any internal doors—the house had just two huge rooms, separated by a long slab of plasterboard or something.

What kind of a crazy shack is this? It's more like a wooden framework than an actual building.

Being a less patient young woman that Hailey Osborne, Teresa Coombs hadn't yet worked out that her wristwatch could also function as a flashlight. Seeing as she had turned off the lights after ducking into this house, she'd so far been searching through it by the dim glow of the streetlight at the street corner. Now though, she felt sufficiently curious to turn the lights back on.

However, when Teresa stepped up to the switch by the front door, she saw Annette stealthily walking down the street outside.

Her first impression was to charge outside and stab the woman, but caution won out over rage. For one thing, Annette had an arrow notched in her bow, with the bowstring pulled taut as if she was ready to shoot at someone. For another thing, Teresa saw that Annette had retrieved her own dropped axe from the floor and had stuck it down the side of her bikini bottom.

Teresa's index finger was poised an inch from the light switch. She withdrew it and instead watched Annette, who now paused, took aim and let the arrow fly.

A few seconds later Teresa heard a male howl of pain from the farther end of the street and then silence. There was no monitor nearby and so she couldn't see what had happened to the man, but Annette's cold smile of triumph and the way she next strode confidently in his direction told Teresa enough.

Well, I guess that's one less suitor to worry about tonight, Teresa mused to herself.

She parted the drapes wider and watched Annette walk towards the man she'd shot. Once Annette had vanished from view, she settled down to plan her own strategy.

Action. She had to act. She couldn't hide in here while the others were out fighting. Unfortunately, she was no longer as armed and dangerous as she would have liked to be.

After a minute's pause, enough time for the deadly Annette to have left the street, Teresa cracked the door open and peered out. The night was empty. Wishing she had a fur coat to cover her bikini, she stepped outside.

She headed in the same direction as Annette had. As she walked, her mind filled with impressions of the arrangement of the game zone. It was an impressive sprawl of buildings, but now she understood that at least two thirds of the buildings were mock-ups, merely existing to create the illusion of a town. This intent was most obvious when, like now, she found herself walking between two rows of shops, with each row being flanked by residential bungalows on either side. In this case the real houses were the four residences, the shops were frame buildings that contained very little in the way of furniture. She also estimated the entire game zone to be about the size of three city blocks placed side by side.

Which indeed was a lot of space to play hide and seek in.

"Well, keep hiding, biatches, I'm seeking."

But she didn't really have much time to either ruminate or bolster her courage. Stepping quickly along the sidewalk, she'd reached the suitor that Annette had shot.

The man was pinned to a tree by an arrow between his eyes. The arrow stuck up like a horn from the forehead of his mask, and blood had leaked from below the mask to run down his neck.

But this was merely the cause of his death. Annette had also mutilated the suitor's corpse.

In addition to the arrow that had pinned his head to the tree, she'd hacked the man's belly completely open so that his intestines had spilled out of him. The looped red mess was draped over his codpiece, hiding it from view.

Teresa refused to be scared or intimidated by the sight. This seemed even more violent than the video of Rhianna's killing that brunette girl last year.

Damn, none of these biatches are fooling around. Alright, girls, I can be evil too.

She dropped to her knees and searched the grass around the man's feet for whatever weapon he'd been holding.

I don't believe it! That biatch Annette must have taken his machete or knife too. How damn selfish can you get!

She felt frustrated. Faced with the sort of violence Annette was bringing to the show, her single knife seemed very inadequate.

Teresa was so intent on her search that she only heard the rush of approaching footsteps when they'd almost reached her.

"Hello, babe, looks like you're my date for the evening," a male voice said near her head.

Shit! She leapt to her feet, swinging her knife with intent to sink it into male flesh. But the man easily grabbed her wrist and painfully slapped the knife from her grasp.

She was still wondering at how easily he'd disarmed her, when he produced a set of handcuffs from somewhere and handcuffed her to himself.

This suitor was very muscular, and even without the handcuffs restraining her, she stood no chance whatsoever of fighting him off. Besides, he had a huge knife of his own, while her own knife lay three feet away on the sidewalk.

"Hey, man, let me go!' she protested. Being restrained like this, her right hand connected to his left wrist, seemed extremely undignified; like she was being arrested by a bounty hunter.

He ignored her. "Damn, you killed Jimmy," he said, regarding the dead man through his mask's eye-holes and scratching his chin under its long black beak. "You really did a number on him."

"Man, *I* didn't kill him. Look at me. Your dead friend's got an arrow through his head and I ain't carrying a bow. All I had was a knife and . . ." She fell silent, letting him figure out the rest for himself.

The suitor laughed and flexed his muscles for her benefit. "Oh, Jimmy ain't my friend. I just recognized the guy by the tattoo on his right arm."

Teresa checked out the corpse's arm and saw the tattoo, a Texas flag. "He's easy to identify, I guess."

"So if *you* didn't kill Jimmy, then who did?"

"Some biatch named Annette. Pretty as fuck, crazy as fuck too, and I'm sure you'll enjoy fucking her much more than you would me." (Desperation was making Teresa rant) "So let me go and go after her instead!" She lowered her voice. "Hey, how 'bout if we make a deal?"

"What deal?"

"You uncuff me and I'll help you catch Annette. She's got great boobs. You'll utterly love her."

The suitor felt Teresa's left breast and pinched her nipple. "Your boobs aren't bad either, babe, and you know what they say . . . about 'a breast in hand being worth two in the bra?' "

Teresa scowled at him. She'd almost thought he'd go for her plan, but staring down at his throbbing erection in his codpiece, she figured it was a dumb hope. "C'mon, man, gimme a break here. Set me free!"

He laughed. "Now, now, babe, you know that isn't gonna happen. All you can do now is keep quiet, 'cept you want your first sexual experience to be a gangbang."

Teresa shivered at his words; their meaning very easy to understand. If she yelled, other suitors would come and then each would claim a share of Teresa's virginity. Her captor didn't want this, as it would mean him splitting his bounty with the others, and he was hoping Teresa would play along, as her doing so would mean her taking on just him and not four or five randy guys.

Teresa had no desire to be gangbanged. She kept quiet. She stole another glance at the man's stiff penis.

At least it ain't too big. Hopefully it won't hurt too much when he enters me. I sure hope it won't. Hey, Miriam, do we get K-Y, or at least Vaseline?

She felt like crying; the tears welled hot to the surface of her face, but she blinked them back. *Oh heck, I can't believe I've been captured so easily.*

"Now, babe," the suitor said, "you and me are just gonna take a walk to somewhere nice and quiet, where we won't be disturbed."

After a final shake of the head at the dead man, Teresa's captor set off between the houses and pulled her after him.

Teresa began scheming. She'd realized she wasn't out for the count yet.

There's still a chance that I can get the keys to these handcuffs away from him and then . . .

She put those thoughts on hold and instead paid attention to her surroundings. They were walking past an empty swimming pool. In the light from the nearby houses, Teresa could see the cracked blue tiles at its bottom, with thick grass growing in the cracks. She toyed with the idea of pushing her captor, who was walking right by the pool's edge, over the poolside when they reached its deep end, but then she realized that if she did so, the handcuffs connecting them would ensure she'd follow him down to the bottom, where they'd most likely break their necks together.

She instead asked him, "Where the hell are you taking me?"

"A nice house on Number Two Street. Place has a nice waterbed, which you're gonna love. Pretty girl like you should lose her innocence in a bed like that, not on some dirty floor."

"What difference does the location make?" Teresa petulantly asked as they left the swimming pool behind and walked down a short alleyway. She realized that until she checked the map on her watch she was as good as lost. "Yeah, what good does a different location do me? You're still gonna . . ."

He nodded, his beaked head dipping like that of a chicken pecking up kernels of corn. "Well, five years from now, when you think back on your first time, which memory would you prefer?"

"All I'm gonna remember is how I didn't win this damn contest."

"Well, tough luck, babe. Your loss is my gain. But I'll go easy on you, and maybe later you'll thank me for it."

"Thank you for what? For . . . ?" She'd been about saying 'for raping me?' but she knew that wasn't the case here. *I signed up for this shit and so . . .*

As if reading her mind, the man said, "Well, don't blame me, cutie pie. You signed up for this shit, just like I . . . Hush!"

Teresa, recalling the consequences of any other suitors joining this one, instantly kept quiet. She heard footsteps coming their way. Then her captor dragged her back out of the alley and through the front door of the nearest house.

"We'll just keep quiet in here for a few minutes, until it's safe outside," he said, taking up a position behind the door. "Then we'll go find that nice, sweet waterbed I mentioned and get this over with." His voice was strained now, as if his balls had begun aching fiercely. Teresa almost sympathized with him. For him to be hard for so long meant he'd have to have taken some 'boner pills,' maybe lots of Viagra or something even stronger. She was also familiar with the caution while using Viagra, which warned users to seek medical assistance if you had an erection for longer than four hours.

Which is clearly why the duration of The Virgin show is three hours.

There was something quite absurd about this situation and Teresa tried not to laugh. What she was thinking was: *This guy is going to all this trouble just to earn two hundred grand, while I, being the virgin here, stand to earn fifty times that much if I can stop him having me and avoid those others too.*

The thought of how much money she stood to earn if she could simply get free now firmed her resolve to try to escape from this man.

Standing there by the front door, she began looking around the building they'd entered. Here the lights were on and she instantly saw that she was once more inside one of the faked buildings, only this one clearly wasn't residential; rather it was a storehouse of some kind. This front room was very large and its walls were covered with shelves on which sat containers of different shapes and sizes.

However, with her wrist bound to the suitor's, looking behind her was easier thought of than done, and soon, growing tired of her constant swiveling about, the man turned and angrily whispered: "Hey, calm down, babe—I can still hear someone out there. What the hell are you so damn antsy about anyway? You want lots of dicks in you?"

"This place," she replied in a whisper, "what is it?"

He shrugged. "It's one of the construction workshops, where they keep all the stuff they need to build and renovate the town. He gestured across the front room with a well-muscled arm. "Power tools, chemicals—acids and stuff like that—floor and ceiling tiles, doors and window frames; you name it, they've got it in here somewhere." He shrugged again. "There are three or four other buildings like this around the game zone. I think one of 'em's right next to the chapel on Number Four Street."

Teresa dully noted the location of that other workshop and of the chapel too (in case she later needed to use it), but her mind had already begun swimming through the possibilities of this place. Tools, chemicals . . . the mention of acids particularly interested her. Unfortunately, all that great harmful stuff was apparently kept in the rear room. Most of what was available out here were stacks of two-by-fours and ceramic tiles, sheets of wallboard, and lots of cartons on the shelves at the room's farther end.

But wait . . . There *were* several bottles of clear fluids on a shelf twelve feet away, but they were unlabeled. And besides, her arms weren't long enough to reach them, except if her captor stepped into the middle of the room; and this brute of a man she was tethered to showed no sign of leaving his position near the door.

She sighed when he said, "Alright, the coast is clear, let's leave."

She checked her watch. *I've only been in the game for forty-two minutes now. I gotta get away from this guy, and I've got only about ten minutes to figure out how to escape from him. Once he gets me on that waterbed of his . . .*

He turned back to her and she sensed him grinning at her behind his bird-mask. "Don't be frightened, cutie-pie. Soon you and I will be in a nice perfumed bed. You only lose your virginity once and I promise to make this first time really special for you."

"Thanks, man," Teresa said. "I really appreciate your doing this for me. It's good to know that someone here actually cares about us girls, because I'm certain that most of the other suitors think of us as meat to be used and discarded, like we don't have any emotions at all. Yeah, I know this is a contest, but we're women and we do all have feelings. So thanks for going to all this trouble to make tonight special for me. Yeah, sure, I'm losing the prize money, but money ain't everything, right? And maybe you're right and in five years time I'll really be grateful that you were so caring about how you deflowered me."

She nodded demurely and looked resigned to her fate. However, inside she was scheming, her mind boiling over with different plans of escape.

I've got just ten minutes to get away from this ape. There has to be a way out of this mess, but what is it?

CHAPTER 11

Hailey & Jessica

House to house to house to house.

Hailey had been tracking two suitors down No. 3 Street. The men's masks meant she couldn't tell for certain, but they seemed to be the same two who'd passed her a while earlier when she'd been hiding behind the tree.

Anyway, she was following them. She figured that if they separated for a while, she could neutralize one or both of them, knock them out or tie them up, which would put them out of the game.

Only I still don't have any duct tape, so I'll need to improvise. And I don't want to have to stab anyone again.

Hailey was moving very quietly, taking care not to be heard. Most of the house lights were on around here, so she was forced to dash from shadowed doorway to porch side, to tree cover. She was being careful to remain about two houses behind the suitors. At this distance she couldn't hear what they were saying; which she felt meant they wouldn't be able to hear her either. So far her tactics had worked.

I just wish they'd split up. Staring at such tight naked male asses is turning me on!

This was of course understandable. This show was about having or not having sex. Like it or not, there came a day when every virgin had to spread her legs and hope for the best. Hailey understood as much. Seeing such sexy men, her natural desire was to surrender herself to them and let them have their way with her. But there was also the prize money to consider. So she must resist her own instincts. She would control herself, no matter what, and put up one hell of a fight if cornered.

The two men had reached the start of No. 3 Street, and were staring across the road at the brick wall that encircled the game zone.

While watching them, Hailey began to have a creepy feeling that someone was watching her too. She also realized that she'd been so intent on not being heard by the men she was following that she'd overlooked something important.

There's something I should have noticed when I walked past it, but which I didn't. Something I saw from the corner of my eyes a short while ago. But what the hell was it? It was across the street, that I'm certain of.

The two men turned the corner and began walking towards No. 2 Street. Hailey however, waited. Once sure the two suitors were too far away to hear her footsteps, she dashed across the road to stand in the shadows cast by the front porch of the first house.

The street was silent, but Hailey wasn't deceived. She waited.

About a minute later, a light came on in the third house on her side.

She grinned. *Bingo! I knew it! Someone's hiding over there. That light must've switched off while the suitors were walking past the building and I wasn't paying any attention either.*

Though still pumped up with the desire to be an active participant in the show, Hailey cautioned herself. *But who's in there? I don't want to tangle with Rhianna or Annette, but I should be able to handle Jessica or Teresa. So I'll just sneak up to the house first and have a look around.*

She hurried across to the third house and began peeking in through its windows. With the lights on she could see everything inside the building. This was another fake-house, a large partitioned space without doors; no ceiling, lots of cartons and debris scattered everywhere and only the barest minimum of furniture. The house did have an outfitted kitchen and a bed in the back room, but little else.

Working from back to front, Hailey looked through all the southern windows, before finally stepping quietly up onto the unscreened front porch for a look into the living room.

Yes, rich girl Jessica Fox was sitting in the living room, in an armchair reminiscent of the one that had earlier released the rattlesnake at Hailey. Jessica's armchair didn't appear to be booby-trapped though; she must have been in the house for a while now, and the chair still looked normal.

Jessica looked relaxed. In fact, she looked better than relaxed. Her right hand was down on her crotch and she was masturbating. Her lips were parted and she was gasping with delight.

Oh, what a slut! Hailey thought with envy, wishing she too felt confident enough to get herself off with danger all around.

She quickly formulated a plan. At the moment, Jessica was completely out of it; she should be easy to overpower and tie up. The platinum blonde's machete lay on the floor between her feet and she was sliding her fingers faster and faster beneath her G-string and her moans were growing deeper and becoming carnal growls. She flung her head around, tensed her legs and shut her eyes.

"Oh, yes, yes, baby—give me that big hard cock! I need it so much!" she gasped, making Hailey wonder what she was doing on *The Virgin* show.

Direct action is best here, Hailey decided. *Just rush in and surprise her. Scare her with my axe so she doesn't put up a fight. The doors don't lock here and so . . . clobber her over the head and knock her out. Sorry 'bout your orgasm, dear, but that's how it goes.*

She flung the front door open and axe raised, charged Jessica.

Then she discovered that Jessica Fox had been faking; that the silver-haired beauty had merely set a trap for her.

Hailey didn't notice the grease and oil smeared on the living room floor until she was right in the middle of it, by which time her velocity had made her lose her balance, so that she went skidding across the room with a collision as the only possible outcome.

Oh no! she thought as she approached the wall opposite the front door.

Hailey first smacked her head against the wall, then against the wooden floor too when she fell to the ground. Her axe went flying off somewhere out of sight, while she lay there half-stunned, wondering where all the stars in her head had come from.

Beside her, Jessica looked up from her masturbation for a moment, nodded at the half-comatose girl beside her, and then with a sensual smile on her lips, skillfully brought herself to a very satisfying sexual climax.

***

24-year-old Jessica Fox was simply another spoiled-rotten rich girl who was dying of boredom.

Her family was so rich that one week they'd all wiped their asses with hundred dollar bills because they ran out of their favorite brand of tissue paper, and they'd also used shredded money as confetti during Jessica's brother Ronald's wedding.

Miriam had selected Jessica mainly because the girl reminded her of herself. She also found it interesting that a girl from such a wealthy family had managed to keep her virginity into her twenty-fifth year. Knowing from experience the way the super-rich operated, by now Jessica ought to have been married off to an equally rich young man and have begun producing the next generation of multimillionaires.

Jessica's psychological profile said she was boringly normal, but Miriam had intuitively questioned this. If nothing else, she thought Jessica Fox must have deep-rooted daddy issues.

It didn't hurt none that Jessica Fox was also drop-dead gorgeous, with a body to match, and with breasts that a porno star would pay a fortune to duplicate. (Jessica's perfect breasts were of course implants, but what was money for, if not to be spent on physical perfection?)

Miriam greatly approved of Jessica Fox. And she'd been certain that her show's viewers would share her opinion. Miriam knew that once they'd gazed upon this particular virgin's physical assets, most of her male audience would be salivating and wishing they too could be 'suitors' on the show.

***

The stars kept swirling around Hailey's internal universe. She was vaguely aware of being hauled to her feet and then half-carried and half-dragged into one of the house's rear rooms. Then she was flung down onto something soft against which she bounced. The bouncing jiggled her brain back to full awareness.

She focused. She was lying on the bed in the back room. Jessica was standing by the bed and staring down at her. She was also holding her machete again.

"Okay, girl, I'm giving you a fair choice," Jessica said, pointing the machete at Hailey. "Fingers or knife? Pick one."

"What are you talking about?" Hailey asked, pushing herself up till she was sitting on the edge of the bed.

Jessica smirked down at her, looking at once both impossibly beautiful and impossibly cruel. "I'm about eliminating you from this competition," she said. "And I'm giving you only two options by which to quit it—either my fingers inside your pussy or my machete inside your guts. It's your choice. Now will you lie still and let me deflower you, in which case you'll live; or am I going to have to hurt you?" She spoke with just the barest suggestion of a drawl; her voice sounded like it had been polished with money.

"Fingers," Hailey instantly replied. Jessica had a look in her eyes which said she wasn't fooling about here. Hailey didn't doubt that the other girl would butcher her without hesitation if she resisted.

And of course I'm gonna resist. I just can't let her know that. I need to keep her talking so I can find a weapon.

"What the hell do you need the money for?" she asked. "You're already rich."

Jessica paused for a moment, tucked the machete beneath her left arm, and began counting off on her fingers. "What do I need the money for? Now let's see: Okay, firstly I need a new bimmer, 'cos my mom borrowed my current one to go shopping and her damn poodles pissed all over the backseat and now I can't get the reek of poodle-pee out of the car no matter what I do. Then I need some new platinum jewelry, and oh yes, one or two plastic surgery procedures that my wealthy dad refuses to pay for and my mom agrees with him, because I'm not married yet and she thinks I should wait till after I've had children to have them." She shrugged at Hailey. "So now you know. Alright, spread your damn legs and let's get this over with."

"Hey, have you ever done this before? I mean, broken another girl's hymen?"

Jessica rolled her eyes. "No, I haven't, stupid. I'm not a dyke. But after signing up for this show I did some online research and also found a video, so I know what I'm doing . . . well, I think I do."

"Wow, that really fills me with confidence."

Jessica pulled the machete from beneath her arm again. "Look, I can always just stab you; either way you'll be out of the show. I won't stab you deep, just enough so you'll be no further threat to me."

Hailey's eyes widened in fear. "Hey, don't you dare stab me! I've already agreed to cooperate."

Jessica growled at her angrily. "So damn well cooperate then and don't act difficult." Her eyes flickered down at her watch. "It's almost the end of the first period, so don't you dare try stalling. Start by pulling your G-string off."

"Hey, I'm just scared of the pain."

"Who isn't? I get so horny each time Donny is kissing and caressing me and I want him deep inside me, but then I get so scared that he's gonna hurt me badly and I'll hate him afterwards for doing so and I push him away and . . . Shit, I've often wondered if I should just get completely drunk and then let him have me that way. But a lady's first time is supposed to be memorable, right, and I don't want to be so out of it that I don't even recall him being inside me. I mean what point is there, waking up next morning with my pussy sore and cum all over my thighs and I don't even remember getting fucked? And it's the *first* time too?"

Jessica glanced sideways at a sudden noise and Hailey leapt off the bed at her. Either she'd timed it just right or Heaven was smiling on her, because she caught Jessica off balance. Jessica dropped her machete and she and Hailey wound up on the floor.

It turned into a catfight, with both young woman rolling over the bedroom floor, banging into cartons left and right and throwing punches and howling in pain as they each yanked on the other's hair.

"I'm gonna kill you, you bitch!"

"No, I'm gonna kill you!"

Jessica was as strong and well-toned as a racing horse, but Hailey was as desperate as a cornered cougar and soon she'd managed to roll on top of Jessica and was banging her head on the wooden floor. Once, twice, thrice and Jessica went all limp and her eyes rolled up in her head.

Panting, Hailey stood up. There was only one thing to do now:

Do unto Jessica as she would do unto me! I'm going to deflower her and then she can go back home to Donny and she won't be worried now that he's going to hurt her. Hey, once she's knocked up she'll even write and thank me for helping her fix her little problem.

But Hailey knew that once she got Jessica's G-string off and put a finger inside her, Jessica was certain to wake up again and their fight would resume. And besides, though she meant to penetrate Jessica and by so doing eliminate her from the competition, she didn't want to hurt her too badly.

And also, as Hailey too didn't have any real idea of how to go about a virgin's defloration, she needed some time to figure things out. *Do I just stick my fingers inside her? And how many of them?* She knew some hymens were reputed to be quite stubborn and that there might also be some bleeding and she wasn't looking forward to it at all.

She stared down at the gorgeous young woman lying at her feet. *Oh, I so wish I had a dick now! It would make this so much easier! How can something so natural be so hard to figure out?*

Anyway, as far as Hailey could see, the only thing to do now was to tie Jessica up and gag her while she did the deed. Binding Jessica would also give her time to work out the proper procedure for what she wanted to do, and would also prevent Jessica from carrying out a revenge on her for kicking her out of the competition.

She began looking around for some rope or duct tape, quickly opening up the few boxes in the back room but finding none. She stepped over Jessica's body, and looked behind the bed, then stepped back over her again to go search outside in the front room.

Then for a moment she paused. *Hey, there's hidden cameras in here recording all this!*

Then Jessica groaned and Hailey forgot all about the cameras. Noting that the other girl's right hand was quite close to her dropped machete, she picked up the machete for her own use.

It isn't like you'll be needing it anymore.

Hailey was once more about leaving the back room when she realized that she'd not yet checked out one particular box at the foot of the bed for duct tape. She tried to get this box open, but it was half-wedged under the bed, so she knelt down to pull it out.

She placed the machete on the bed, then took a firm grip on the stuck box and tugged. The box came free and Hailey swayed back with it. But at that same moment, she glimpsed a thin cord jerk free and streak away towards the wall.

Oh damn, it's booby-trapped! The carton was holding the rope down!

Instantly throwing down the box, Hailey leapt as far away from the bed as she could. Then she looked back and cringed.

A chamber in the top half of the left bedroom wall (the wall beside the bed) had popped open. And a lot of large, black and hairy creatures were pouring out of it. Hailey's initial thought was 'rats,' but these rats seemed to have too many legs.

Then she saw that they were giant spiders. Giant black spiders, some of them as big as her fist.

Unfortunately for Jessica, she'd been standing over Hailey with the machete raised. Hailey had had no idea that Jessica had revived and now she'd never know what the platinum-blonde beauty had intended to do to her with the raised machete. Because, standing at that particular point at the foot of the bed put Jessica directly in line with the emptying hole in the bedroom wall.

And the spiders swarmed all over her.

Jessica went down again; this time screaming as the black mass of spiders covered her body. She hit the floor and began thrashing and swinging the machete about as if the air was the enemy she was fighting with. Then her cries of fear and agony turned to soft moans of anguish as the spiders bit her and injected their paralyzing venom into her body. The spiders ran back and forth over Jessica and even over each other, fighting one another in their desperation to reach her soft flesh.

Hailey could only watch in horror. She felt numb, as if the spiders had tranquilized her too. A portion of her mind urged her to go to Jessica's rescue; but there was no way that she was stepping into that black arachnid mass.

Hell no! That isn't about happening, no matter what!

Hailey only jerked out of her paralysis when she felt something scratchy on her leg. She looked down and saw that one of the giant spiders was nuzzling at her right ankle, investigating her warm body with its legs to see if she was another potential meal.

With a shudder she kicked the beastly thing away. It flew across the room and landed on the bed, from where it dropped down onto Jessica's body and quickly forced its way down through the others.

Jessica's head broke out from the black mass. Her pale eyes were glazed—she looked drugged, totally spaced-out. Her skin was a mass of bites, her face swollen worse than if she'd stuck her head into a beehive. Her head submerged again into the black mass. An equally bitten and swollen hand emerged then also vanished. The spiders bubbled in a seemingly enraged frenzy over her.

Hailey managed not to scream while watching all this; but her silence was only because she was scared of calling the giant spiders' attention to herself.

I'd better leave now before they realize I'm in here too.

Stepping carefully so that the spiders wouldn't notice her, Hailey moved along the wall to the doorway and exited into the front room. Then, after looking around for her dropped axe and grabbing up the knife she found instead of it, she ran out of the house.

Behind her, she imagined she could hear Jessica Fox silently screaming for help.

She began wondering how she could summon help for the girl, but then, arriving at the next street monitor, she saw a glorious HD-color replay of everything she'd just been through, and realized she needn't worry—help for Jessica must already be on the way.

CHAPTER 12

Teresa

"Okay, looks like the coast is clear now," the suitor said and pulled the door open. Then he tugged Teresa after him. The set of handcuffs joining them hurt her wrist and she was about to protest about him yanking so hard on it, when . . .

The new man appeared so suddenly that it was only afterwards that Teresa worked out that he must have been hiding beside the door. The entranceway jutted out about a foot and a half from the house, and the man must have waited silently by the side of this projecting part until Teresa's captor was ready to leave the building.

Anyway, like a bird of prey, the man was suddenly there in front of both of them. His machete gleamed in a brilliant flash of silver and punctured a hole in Teresa's captor's belly, and then, when that man staggered back and tried lifting his own machete to defend himself, his attacker's machete took off his right arm at the shoulder.

The violence occurred so fast that it was over almost before it had begun. One moment Teresa was being yanked out through the door, and the next she was being propelled back through it again, this time under the force of her dying companion's own reverse motion as a third swipe of the attacker's machete almost cut his head completely off his neck.

Teresa lost her balance and hit the floor. Her fall helped pull her captor down on top of her, and she lay there, more confused than afraid. She felt the man lying on her tremble and groan out his death agonies, until finally, with a violent shake of his torso he gave up the ghost and lay still and heavy on her.

She lay motionless under him. For the moment, her mind had emptied itself of everything except self-preservation.

Then her new captor stepped inside the storage house and waved at her.

"Hi pretty," he said brightly, flicking blood off his machete. "I'm glad I'm finally meeting you in person. I've had your pussy on my mind ever since I first set my eyes on you in the Control Center."

"Hi, there," Teresa managed to mouth back at him. She had to admit that he did look impressive standing there naked with just that plague mask and mesh codpiece on. He was tall and powerfully built, and if anything, more muscular than the dead man, with of course the ubiquitous erection they all had.

She expected him to immediately lock the door behind him, but he didn't. Instead, he waved down at her again. "Hold on a bit, sweetie, while I clean the blood off the front steps. We don't want anyone disturbing our fun, do we?"

The cheeriness of the man's words brought a sense of reality back to Teresa, who was now quite drenched in the dead man's blood. *No, he's not nuts and neither am I. He's merely playing this game by its rules, and it's time I do so too, if I want to win this thing.*

The man had vanished into the rear room and Teresa heard him humming in there. An upbeat tune that sounded like something by Slain Jane, but she couldn't remember the name of the song. She quickly shook off her questions about how he could be so blasé after just murdering a man. Sliding out from beneath the corpse, she questioned her own calm. She realized that she wasn't upset by the blood that now coated her body; she wasn't revolted by either its smell or its sticky texture. Indeed, except for the fact that she was still chained to this dead man, everything about this bloody scenario felt right to Teresa.

It's just that I ain't yet participating in the damn violence. And she suddenly felt impatient to join in. *Guys and murder dolls, it's about time that I began dishing out some bloodshed of my own.*

"Won't be long now," the suitor announced cheerily, stepping out from the rear room with a mop and a bucket.

His insistence on cleaning up struck Teresa as rather neurotic, but she looked on the positive side of things. His delay in having sex with her just gave her more time to get free. *Where the hell is the key to these handcuffs?*

She'd already realized that the reason her new captor wasn't paying too much attention to her was because she was chained to the dead man, meaning she wasn't about running off.

Where is the key to the handcuffs? She leaned over the corpse to search it and, seen from the front, the sight did make her grimace. *Damn, he sure did a number on you! Aw well, at least your boner's gone down now.*

Two or three coils of intestine protruded from the ripped-up belly, and the way the man's head wobbled when she moved his body . . . as if Teresa could now tear it off with her bare hands.

She fought down the tempting image of trying to manually decapitate the corpse. *I'm running out of time here!* But the temptation was an amusing one, and one which again made her question her own sanity.

A few yards away the new suitor was whistling happily while mopping the blood off the front steps. Now his actions really did strike Teresa as crazy. *Why waste time doing that, when all he has to do is take that damn codpiece off and stick his dick in me?*

She didn't want him to, of course. Everything was just so surreal, that was all. It was like waking up one morning to discover that the American constitution had been repealed and that everything once forbidden was now legal.

And as she finally began searching the dead man for the handcuff keys, she was unconsciously coming to terms with the idea that on this show she could actually do anything that came to her mind to anyone she wanted to do it to. And more dangerously now, another, unconscious thought stream was unlocking her large catalogue of irritations—her suppressed feelings of being put down, of being misunderstood, her endless fears of being sexually abused by her drunk of a father (which had never happened), her feelings of insecurity, her worries that she'd never amount to more than her washed-out mother and older sisters had. All the negativity and hatreds that society had helped her repress to make her into a good and upright citizen were being forced to the surface.

Teresa's subconscious abruptly made the psychic hookup to this unconscious runaway train of rages, and all of a sudden, she UNDERSTOOD . . . actually UNDERSTOOD that, *Well, here I can do what-the-fuck-ever I want to.*

And when that understanding hit her, Teresa Coombs smiled without understanding why.

She couldn't find the key. She'd assumed that it had to be on the dead suitor and had checked the two most logical places for him to have secured it: his codpiece and his mask. Checking the latter had meant loosening its straps and viewing his face—he was very handsome; maybe she'd have enjoyed losing her virginity to him after all.

But she'd not found the key. There was one final possible hiding place, but even though she knew everyone on the show had been cleared for diseases, Teresa had no intention of sticking her fingers up anyone's ass and fishing around in there. She rolled the dead man over on his side, parted his buttocks and stared angrily at his hairy anus.

"Nah, I don't think it's up his ass either," the new suitor said. "I think he just threw it away, knowing that the guards would release you once you were out of the contest."

She jerked around and gaped at him. She hadn't realized that he'd finished his cleanup.

He propped the mop and bucket against the wall. "Okay, sweetie, now that everywhere's nice and clean, let's get your pussy nice and wet and red. Alright, get up."

Teresa cringed at his words. She got to her feet, but the dead man kept her tethered in place. The guy had to weight at least 220 pounds and he was all dead weight. She looked longingly at the shelf with the bottles of clear liquid, wishing she was a yard or two nearer to them. Oh, if she could just make it to one of those bottles and splash this guy with its contents. But what if the bottles only contained vinegar? Or olive oil or denatured alcohol?

The suitor tapped his machete on his thigh; the other machete lay just inside the front door, a few inches from the fingers of the dead man's severed arm. Staring at the discarded weapon, Teresa felt frustrated enough to scream for help.

She didn't scream though. She still didn't wish to be gangbanged.

"Okay, now let's get you comfortably set up," the suitor said in a voice brimming over with glee.

To Teresa, this statement was more evidence that this guy was a loony of some kind. At the very least he was mentally retarded.

Maybe they all are? Or why else would this guy—she glanced down at the corpse she was chained to—*want to take me to a 'nice soft waterbed' when he could've had me on the grass by the sidewalk? And now this man too?*

"Er . . . I need to get this guy off me first," she told the suitor, indicating the handcuffs.

He shook his head, the action so much like that of a bird looking around that she wished he wasn't wearing that silly, creepy plague mask. "No need to," he replied. "I like you restrained like this. You can use the guy as a pillow."

This looked to be it then for Teresa's hymen. She gaped in fear at the suitor's erection, dreading the moment he'd unclip the codpiece and let it out of confinement. To this inexperienced virgin, the stiff penis looked enormous. *Ouch, it's gonna hurt me for sure! I just know I'm gonna bleed like roadkill! Shit!*

Teresa checked her watch. *Dammit, just five minutes till the first rest period, when I'd have a fifteen minute respite. Hey, what's tha—*

"Too much slippery blood over here," the suitor said, grabbing her by the shoulders and breaking up her concentration. "I'll need to move you over somewhere cleaner."

He let go of her shoulders, stepped past her and took a hold of the dead man's left arm instead. "Now I come to think of it, it was real dumb of this jerk to throw the key away." He began hauling the man across the room, which meant Teresa had to follow along too.

But she didn't mind being moved like this, past those bottles of clear liquid that she'd once considered her sole chance of salvation. She'd noticed something even better on the shelves she was being pulled towards.

A yellow box cutter/utility knife lay between two cartons, its short blade gleaming invitingly. The guy hauling the dead guy was facing the other way and so hadn't seen it, and in a few seconds, if they kept going, Teresa's fingers would be able to reach it.

And then they did. Her only worry as her fingers wrapped around the box cutter's grip was that she was right-handed but the damn handcuffs were making her use her left hand for this.

"Alright, we're fine over here," the suitor said, straightening up again. "Now, sweetie, how d'you want it, face to face or doggy-style? But remember doggy-style shortens the pussy, making the cock go in deeper and since this is your first time doing it, that might hurt a lot."

"How 'bout if I take a rain check?" Teresa said, feeling an intense burst of pleasure as she stabbed him with the box cutter. She jabbed the short blade into his belly as deep as it would go, then swiftly ripped it across his perfect abs. This took more strength than she'd expected it would and she almost dropped the blade as his blood drenched her fingers. But she held on and got the deed done.

"Ooooooh, you bitch!" he howled and swung his machete at her. But the pain in his belly meant he couldn't concentrate and besides, Teresa stepped in close to him and, with a rush of brute strength she shoved him hard against the shelves and stuck the box cutter into his side again, this time ripping down towards his crotch until the codpiece halted the blade's progress.

Still howling, the suitor dropped his machete and tried grappling with Teresa, now grabbing her shoulders and trying to push her off him. But she held on and stabbed him in the chest.

Her strength was born of sheer desperation and the knowledge that now she was fighting for her life—that this guy was certain to butcher her too if he got the upper hand here. But at the same time, she felt a huge joy at shedding his blood. By now she was covered in his blood too and more spilled from each fresh hole she made in his previously perfect body. The long beak of his plague mask prodded her in the head, and glancing up at him, she had a moment's terrifying impression that she was battling a creature like the ancient Minotaur of Greek legend. This impression spurred her to greater violence; a monster had no need of her compassion.

He finally shoved her off of him and cocked his fist and punched her in the face. The blow stunned her a little, but she ducked underneath his follow-up punch and stabbed him in the neck, getting him right underneath the strap that held his mask in place. She thrilled as the blade went into his skin, ripping it hard across his throat and finally hacking it down into the muscles over his heart. At the same time she dug the fingers of her right hand into the hole she'd made in his belly and grabbed firm hold of his intestines and squeezed hard and did her utmost best to tear them out of him.

He hit her another blow, this time catching her on the side of the head, and this one really did stun her, so that her gaze dimmed, her eyes crossed and she staggered back from him and leaned against the wall. But he was already dead on his feet. He was a bloody wreck now, bleeding from half a dozen tears and gashes across his torso, and with blood gushing from his ripped-open throat.

Blearily, she watched the eyes in his mask glaze over. Then she slumped down to the floor, seconds before he too collapsed face-first onto the other suitor's corpse.

She sat there with her back against the cartons on the lowest shelf, drenched in the man's blood and breathing heavily. Though dazed, she was very satisfied with what she'd just done. She had just protected her virginity. And it had felt great doing so.

***

Teresa sat there for she didn't know how long, but jerked to full alertness when the front door opened.

Dammit, not another suitor! You'd think I was the only virgin on the show! She quickly felt around her for the dead man's machete. Once she'd found it she took a firm grip on it and waited. Once more she regretted only being able to use her left hand.

But it wasn't the suitors. It was a pair of guards. One male, one female. Red gloves and boots, dark blue jumpsuits and those motorbike helmets that completely hid their faces.

"First rest period," the female guard called out as they approached. "Fifteen minutes of no combat." Then she apparently got a good look at the two corpses because she added, "Fuck! You're really givin' your all, girl."

Teresa waved her machete at the pair and nodded. "Yeah. So what you guys here for?" She realized that her watch must have vibrated for recess but she'd been too dazed to notice the signal.

"You hungry or thirsty?" the male guard asked. "We got a cart of hotdogs, burgers, and ice-cold Cokes and Pepsis outside."

"Sandwiches and cold milk too, if you prefer those instead," the female guard added. "The sandwiches are veggie."

Teresa shook her head. "No food, thanks, but I'd like a cock . . . sorry, I mean a Coke."

And because it was that sort of surreal situation, everyone laughed.

And of course this was the most surreal of circumstances: herself on the floor with her buttocks and breasts dripping with someone else's blood, both of her hands and forearms as red as if she worked in a slaughter house . . . sitting beside two gorily butchered men and yet sharing a joke with a man and a woman dressed like extras from a dystopian sci-fi flick.

If nothing else, it speaks of a temporary lapse in my sanity.

'HYMEN PROTECTION' read the patches on their shoulders. The wording of the logo made her feel a little bit mad.

Teresa said, "What I really need is someone to help me get this damn handcuff off my damn wrist." To make her point she lifted her right hand, which automatically also raised the dead suitor's brawny left arm.

The guards shook their heads. "Sorry, we can't help you out there," the man said. "You gotta figure that one out for yourself."

Teresa gaped at them. "You mean I gotta stay handcuffed to this dead hunk of meat?"

"Not necessarily," the female guard said, then gestured towards the back room. "There may be bolt cutters in the rear storeroom, or a key even."

Teresa scowled and raised her cuffed arm again. "And I'm supposed to drag loverboy here along with me until I find them?"

"Uh huh," the male guard said. "That's the general idea."

"Shit! Thanks for nothing, guys."

"Well, I'll go get you that cock . . . sorry I mean Coke, that you wanted."

This time the joke fell flatter than stale Coke. No one laughed. The man strode off to the front door.

"What now?" Teresa asked his female partner. "Are you guys gonna remove the bodies?" She gestured at the butchered corpses beside her. "My butt feels glued to the floor by all this blood everywhere."

The other woman shook her head. "Not till the show's over. Just two hours to go."

Teresa shrugged the information off. "Hey," she asked the woman, her face reflected in the black helmet's visor, "have you ever competed on this show? Or wanted to?"

"I'd have liked to, but I never had a chance. Lost my virginity when I was fourteen. Guitar player friend of my brother's—they had a band, used to rehearse in our garage and drive mom mad with the noise 'cos they were really bad." Her voice turned dreamy with memory. "He was super-cute, had curly blonde hair and the loveliest blue eyes you'd ever seen. Anyway, one night he kissed me and I couldn't resist and went the *hole* way with him." She laughed as the male guard reappeared with Teresa's drink. "I don't remember it hurting much, but I bled like . . . and was sore for the next two days. I was glad afterwards that I'd gotten it out of the way though. Was something to brag about to the other girls at school."

The man handed Teresa a Coke in a Big Gulp-sized cup. She tried to accept it with her right hand, then growled in frustration, dropped the machete and used her left instead.

The Coke *was* ice cold. "Thanks," she said, then slipped the straw into her mouth and took a sip.

Afterwards she checked her watch. *Rest Period One: −8:00,* the screen read.

She took another sip of Coke and stared up at the two guards, her face twice reflected in the black glass of their helmet visors.

"So, we'll be leaving you now," the female guard said. "Good luck with the show. Hope you win."

"Yeah, good luck!" the male guard said. "Remember, there's food in the cafeterias if you change your mind about eating. All the food is safe."

"Yeah, thanks." Teresa waved goodbye at them.

They left Teresa there with her iced cup of Coca-Cola and her two corpses.

"Hey, has anybody quit yet?" she asked as they stepped out of the doorway.

The female guard had already exited, but the male guard turned back to her.

He laughed. "Not unless you count your two dead boyfriends there and Jimmy—that's the Texan guy Annette pinned to the tree with an arrow. Why you asking?"

"Just wanna know how my competition's doing, that's all."

The man laughed again. "Well, if you ladies keep going at this rate, soon you'll have knocked off all the suitors and have to start battling each other for the prize money."

She gestured at the dead men. "There's no replacements then?"

He shook his head. "No. It's considered unfair to you ladies and besides it screws up the betting odds, so the audience don't like it either." He pointed to her arm. "Hey, if you need to keep up with the scores, your watch'll tell you. Just scroll through Options."

"Yeah, okay." She'd forgotten she was wearing a watch. The timepiece was so coated with blood now that it looked like a tumor growing on her arm.

She heard the female guard calling to her partner from outside and the man waved at her. "And hey—once more, good luck."

"Thanks," she called back as he stepped outside.

***

Once her Coke was all gone Teresa was faced with the big problem of how to get free of the man she was chained to.

That woman said there might be bolt cutters or a key in the back room.

So Teresa got to her feet and, hauling the dead man after her, headed that way. She made it as far as the door to the back room before quitting from the effort. But standing there in the doorway was enough. From her vantage point, she could see the entire room, and it was filled with cartons and crates. Stacked floor-to-ceiling with them like a warehouse.

There were too many containers to search through to make the attempt worthwhile. *I could be looking through them for hours!*

By the base of one stack of boxes Teresa noticed a hammer and a hacksaw. She considered dragging the dead man over there and trying them out, but quickly changed her mind.

The hacksaw might get these cuffs off of me, but I ain't got the time to sit here trying to saw them off. Shit, I wish I . . . I . . .

Then she laughed; softly but confidently. Staring down at the dead man, she'd just remembered that he had only one arm. She'd also remembered how that had come about.

And what works once, is most certain to work again.

Grinning to herself, Teresa dragged the dead suitor back over to where she'd been sitting. Once there, she arranged his body so that his left arm lay on the other dead suitor's chest. Then she picked up the machete.

Alright, where do I hack it off from, wrist or elbow?

'Elbow' was quickly discarded, since cutting his arm off there would mean she'd still have to carry his forearm around with her. It would be better to just sever his left hand; then she'd be completely free of him.

While making up her mind, she'd moved her own arm, which had in turn slipped the man's arm out of position. She arranged the man's arm in place again, raised the machete and slammed it down on his wrist.

Her first blow took off his thumb and index finger. She shrugged. It was a lot like chopping up chicken at home, only her left arm wasn't as strong as her right one and she had no experience in handling tools with her left hand.

She hacked again. This time the blade bit deep into the wrist, but then deflected and glanced off the cuff's steel loop.

She winced at the noise. *I'd better be careful, I don't wanna dull its edge.*

Teresa resumed hacking. This time she didn't stop until the dead man's hand dropped completely off his wrist.

CHAPTER 13

Miriam

With the first rest period drawing to a close, Miriam was finally having her long-desired cunnilingus. While her husband Aaron knelt between her legs and sucked on her clitoris, she shut her eyes and floated away on clouds of bliss. As she always did during sex that didn't require her standing up, she'd removed her prosthetic leg. It lay across two of the chairs the virgins had earlier sat on. Miriam always squeezed her thighs tightly against Aaron's head while he licked her and the prosthesis impeded her movement.

The monitors were replaying the most interesting snippets of action from the first game period. Things had really picked up towards the end, with that suitor Teresa had killed, but what everyone really wanted to see was the girls getting fucked, and that hadn't happened yet.

Of course the deflorations would start soon, as everyone grew desperate to claim the prize money. The bloodshed so far had merely whetted the spectator's appetites; now they knew they wouldn't be disappointed; there was sleazy fun on the horizon.

But still, Miriam felt very tense from all the physical and mental energy she'd expended today, and this sex was helping her relax. So she kept her eyes closed and ignored the screen and let herself be pampered by the love of her life.

The two guards previously stationed inside the Control Center now stood outside it grinning to themselves at the loud moans coming through the door.

Miriam's swollen clitoris throbbed with pleasure as her husband tickled it with his tongue. As the delicious sensations spread through her body, she gripped first his hair, then his ears, then his hands as they caressed her breasts through her top, then she just let her hands flop to her sides and gasped and groaned.

Aaron Heller slipped his tongue between Miriam's pale buttocks and licked her anus. While a finger worked on her clitoris, he thinned the oral muscle and stuck its tip through her anal ring. He worked his tongue inside her for a while, twisting it in the loop of her sphincter, and then slid it out again.

Then, swallowing saliva, he leaned back and smiled at his gasping wife. His right hand continued to stimulate her clitoris. His left traced a teasing finger along the seam of fusion at the base of her vaginal petals. He teased and tickled her swollen labia; teasing, teasing, teasing . . . pleasing, pleasing, pleasing . . .

Aaron couldn't slip a finger into Miriam's vagina, because . . . well, Miriam no longer had a vagina.

***

See, after losing her leg at age sixteen, Miriam Oates endured life as well as she could. Though she was very attractive, the missing limb made her shy of dating anyone, so she remained a virgin till she was twenty-four, when her mother died and left her some money. Not much money, but more than enough for what Miriam had been contemplating doing for the past five years.

Once the will had been read, Miriam quickly contacted a surgeon friend who specialized in body modifications. Once they'd agreed on the extent of the procedure and the price, she packed her bags and flew down to Los Angeles.

The procedure Miriam wanted was simple—she had now decided that she wanted her virginity preserved for all time. She had requested both for a hysterectomy and for the total removal of her vagina, complete with its still intact hymen.

The operation was performed and was a success, with the nerves that supplied the sensitive first third of the removed sexual passage being rerouted to her labia instead. The vaginal lips were pulled right next to each other, the vulval opening completely stitched up, and both the removed vagina and womb handed to Miriam in a jar of formaldehyde solution.

That jar was now Miriam Heller's most treasured possession. It sat on an altar of sorts in her bedroom and whenever she was at home she stared at it everyday and felt she received strength from it. She also carried pictures of her removed genitals around with her.

Some might consider this neurotic behavior, but Miriam didn't. She wasn't worshipping her vagina; at least not yet. And even if she was, in some circles her attitude and behavior would not only be considered healthy, but also worthy of emulation. It was definitely in Miriam's favor that nowadays even feminists weren't sure what feminism actually entailed anymore.

Of course, not having a vagina did create some insecurities in Miriam. Once she had fully recovered from the operation, she grew obsessed with finding a man to love her. And to make love to her. To her as to most people, 'being in love' and 'making love' were two inseparable things.

She could still reach orgasm, and very easily at that—her clitoris hadn't been tampered with at all . . . but . . .

But what full-blooded man would want a woman he couldn't penetrate? (Miriam's one trial of anal intercourse had conclusively assured her that the 'back door' wasn't her sexual route.)

Miriam's romantic problem was solved two years later when she met Aaron Heller. Aaron was only the second man who'd not run for the hills on discovering Miriam didn't have a vagina. (The first gentleman was the one who'd suggested they travel the anal route instead.)

When they'd started dating, Aaron Heller had told Miriam that he was only good at two things: "Making money and eating pussy."

Miriam didn't know about Aaron's moneymaking skills, but his prowess in cunnilingus totally floored her. After the first time that he'd gone down on her, which left her crying and thanking him afterwards for being so nice to her 'poor and unworthy body,' she'd decided she wanted him forever.

Thankfully, he felt the same way about her too.

Most important, Aaron was content to settle for a sex life that consisted only of fellatio, hand-jobs and mutual masturbation. Miriam didn't at all mind being titty-fucked, but she had small breasts, so they let that one slide and just gave each other head most of the time.

They kept dating and made plans to get married and soon it was meet-the-parents weekend.

Now, Aaron Heller came from a prominent Jewish family of New York bankers.

Both of his parents initially welcomed Miriam with open arms. The fact that she'd lost a leg only added to their sympathetic outlook.

But then, one night, Aaron had drunkenly confided to his mother about Miriam's other physical modifications. On hearing about her prospective daughter-in-law's missing privates, Mrs. Heller had almost suffered a heart attack.

See, Aaron was an only son and his parents were impatient for him to continue the dynasty. They'd been relieved when he'd brought Miriam home. But now, they wanted her out of their house and out of their son's life immediately.

As Aaron's father patiently explained to him over dinner the next day (Miriam not being present), "Son, you know your mother and I aren't the least bit racist, but if you're going to marry a goy, for Yahweh's sake, marry one who can have kids!"

Aaron, however, was too much in love. He refused to ditch Miriam.

So his parents ditched him instead. To make him see things their way, Aaron was disowned. This was meant to be a temporary measure, merely "till he comes back to his senses."

But the well-meaning parents hadn't counted on their only son being so headstrong . . . or so damn resourceful.

Aaron went on (or off) and married Miriam anyway. And it was while musing on how to make ends meet while access to Aaron's half-a-billion dollars inheritance was tied up for the foreseeable future, that the young Mr. and Mrs. Heller came up with the idea of setting up the Hi, Men! escort agency and hosting *The Virgin* game show.

The rest—as they say—is history. Or in this case, underground internet infamy.

***

Aaron clamped his lips tightly around Miriam's clitoris and stuck the tip of his finger up her ass. Miriam exploded into orgasm, gripping Aaron's dark hair so hard that it felt as if she was yanking it out by the roots. He kept licking and sucking until she relaxed.

"Feel better now, honey?" he asked with that handsome grin of his that she found irresistible.

She nodded limply and then let her head fall back and her hair dangle over the backrest. The images on the surrounding monitors flickered over her like fireworks.

A short while later the buzzer rang for the start of the second game period and Miriam sat up again. She felt as relaxed as if she'd had a nap. Ready to attend to her virgins again.

"What do you think so far?" she asked Aaron as she pulled her prosthetic leg back on. He was sitting with his ankles crossed and his hands clasped in his lap, watching the different replays. The display currently showed Annette Morrison shooting arrows at Rhianna Jackson, who was running faster than a lioness being hunted on safari to escape her. Rhianna finally flung herself through an open window.

Aaron turned to Miriam with a frown on his face. "Maybe we should ban arrows next year. They give one an unfair advantage."

"I disagree, honey," Miriam said, tightening her leg straps. "All the girls had the same weapons options. Any of the others could have picked a bow also. In fact they should have—if they'd been thinking right instead of admiring their hairdos in the mirror they'd have realized that they could carry lots of other stuff in the quiver, not just arrows."

"True," Aaron nodded, smoothing down his dark suit and then indicating the amazon with the bow as she strode towards the house that Rhianna had already exited by the back door. "But Annette didn't take anything but that bow, did she? Or did she also stuff a knife in her quiver?"

Miriam thought on it but couldn't remember. She could request a rewind from the technicians, but that would take time. And she wasn't really interested in Annette's armory anyway.

She sat next to her husband and took his hand in hers. "You haven't answered my question, darling." She gestured up at the screens, which had now switched from their replay to tracking the twelve remaining contestants as they resumed moving. "So . . . what do you think of this year's crop of virgins?"

He shrugged. "You know I leave the appraisals to you. You're the expert on virginity." She laughed at their private joke and he went on, "But of course, from a marketing angle, I can assure you that the show's already broken last year's records, both for viewership and the bets are sky-high too. All the girls are hits with the audience."

Miriam smiled. She was impressed with these women; they were quite a tough bunch; including Hailey, whom she'd not given much of a chance. But so far the young virgin had given a good account of herself.

The screen focused on Jessica Fox, who was still twitching in that back room now that the giant spiders were done with her. Miriam winced on seeing the girl. Jessica looked utterly horrible.

The bugs, however, seemed to have lost interest in her; they were scattered all over the house now, giant spiders walking on the walls and ceiling, spiders spinning webs in corners and across the doorways and windows, spiders eating their way into cartons and then climbing in and out of them. Some spiders lay belly-up on the floor, seemingly dead from their own exertions.

Meanwhile Jessica twitched and trembled on the floor.

"Aaron, where did you get those damn spiders?"

"Guy shipped them up from Belize, if I recall correctly. Or maybe they're from Chile." He too looked at Jessica. "What? You're thinking of sending the guards to bring her in?"

She shook her head. "We can't. It's against the rules. She'll be there for the next two hours, unless . . ."

Aaron nodded. "Unless she either revives enough to continue . . . or the suitors find her."

Miriam frowned and also nodded. The rules of the game were brutal; but they were essential. *The Virgin* was all about character and strength of will. Pussies need not apply.

Three men were already dead. God only knew how many of the twelve remaining contestants would survive, if any.

Miriam's initial idea had been to have the virgins all stand with their weapons raised in the Control Center and make that "We who are about to die, salute you!" declaration from the ancient days of the Roman coliseum, when the gladiators fought against one another and against wild beasts. But Aaron had vetoed it as too melodramatic.

To Miriam, losing one's virginity *was* a sort of death—the death of a woman's innocence . . .

"Hey," Aaron said, noticing her dour mood. "I was just telling you how much of a hit with the audience all of our female contestants are. In fact, Sheik Ibrahim Khomeini jokingly asked if any of them are for sale after the competition ends." He grinned. "The sheik is particularly interested in Rhianna Jackson. He says his harem lacks that distinctive

African-American flavor and that since his nephew Wissam married Janet Jackson he's wanted to acquire a black girl of his own. He specifically asked if Rhianna was in any way also related to Michael Jackson. He's offering five million for her if her hymen's intact; three if she loses it on the show."

Miriam cracked a smile. "That randy old goat; he knows the girls aren't for sale. How the hell does he still get it up? He's almost eighty."

"Think 'Viagra,' honey, and you can hardly go wrong."

The second period was well under way; five minutes in now. Monitors showed blood-drenched Teresa walking with a grim expression on her face, a bloody machete in each hand and a set of handcuffs dangling from her right wrist; Rhianna Jackson ducking through a doorway on No. 2 Street as two suitors turned the corner into the same street; Annette stalking another suitor; Hailey staring in fright and ducking back into hiding as the last four suitors came in a rush up No. 3 Street.

"Hey, something's going on," Aaron said, pointing to the relevant monitor as it locked fully onto this latter group of suitors and expanded its contents across the rest of the LED screens, so that the image was blown up into a giant composite one.

"Yes, those guys do seem very motivated," Miriam agreed. Of course it was impossible to see the men's faces with those plague masks on, but all four of them were stepping with a very determined thread.

Then Aaron laughed. "And you know what street this is, right? I do think we're about to witness our first defloration of the night."

Miriam scowled, feeling the familiar flush of regret that always came when she was about to witness the destruction of female purity. She squeezed her husband's hand and groaned, "And to think that I had such high hopes for that girl. Honey, I told you I selected her mainly because she reminded me of myself at that age."

CHAPTER 14

Hailey

Hailey, who'd spent the recess period snacking on energy bars in the cafeteria up No. 3 Street, had initially been scared that the approaching suitors were coming for her.

But just as she was about to fling away her can of Red Bull and bolt for the cafeteria's rear entrance, the four men had turned off the road into one of the houses.

Hailey quickly realized which house they had entered.

Oh shit, that's where Jessica is!

One thing she was certain of: *Jessica is about to go home to daddy and Donny.*

Hailey now faced a choice: *I can either go down the street to view what is going to happen to Jessica, or I can flee, get out of Dodge while the going is good.*

In the end, her curiosity won out. The cafeteria didn't have a monitor and there wasn't one nearby in the street outside, so Hailey let herself out by the side door and headed down towards the house where she'd fought Jessica. There was a monitor on the wall of the house next to that one, but she'd need to cross the road to be able to view it safely. On this side of the street the suspended image would be too large and too nearby, and she'd also be standing out in the open.

So now I'm a voyeur too, she thought as an unfamiliar excitement filled her, an excitement which oddly seemed to either begin or end in her private parts.

She partly succeeded in shrugging the feeling off, but then quit worrying at her sudden burst of amorality. *This isn't the real world, hon. Real-world terms and conditions don't apply here. I'm watching this and that's that.*

She quickly crossed the road and hid behind the blue sign by a small shed, which, had she been paying closer attention, would have informed her (in beautiful white cursive lettering) that she was standing right beside the No. 3 Street Chapel, where for the next fifteen minutes she was welcome to lay down her burdens and rest.

But Hailey was so burdened with anticipation and so focused on the monitor opposite that she missed even the three white crosses marked on the blue door beside her which indicated the opening of that sanctuary.

Well, now I've got a ringside seat, she thought as the monitor showed the suitors battling the giant spiders that had bitten and stung Jessica into her almost comatose state.

The spiders were delighted at the prospect of fresh human meat and had set upon the four men immediately they'd stepped through the door; but this time the giant arachnids didn't have the element of surprise. The suitors (whom Hailey now realized must have worked out which house Jessica was in from the monitors and then begun a street to street search to find her) had known there were spiders in the building and had come prepared. The bugs swarmed over the men and bit fiercely, but they were battered aside, chopped in pieces, spitted like kebab meat, and stomped into messy puddles of bug flesh, the sight of which made Hailey gag. At one point she thought that the spiders might still prevail, but soon the last of them was crushed beneath a suitor's black Nikes and that was it for them.

Then the four suitors apparently decided that there was too much dead-bug mess inside the house and they picked Jessica up and carried her outside. Two men brought Jessica out of the house; the other two brought out the mattress from the bed in the back room.

Hailey realized that she now *literally* had a ringside seat, as the men put the mattress down right in the middle of the street and placed Jessica on top of it, naked and spread-eagled.

Hailey winced at the sight of her. Jessica was a total mess. Hailey couldn't tell if she was conscious or unconscious, but her skin was riddled with bleeding bites from head to toe and she was twitching, her flesh swollen and purple like she was covered with hives. Her face was turned towards Hailey and she was drooling spittle in a continuous stream from the left corner of her open mouth. Jessica's gray eyes were wide open and staring straight ahead of her and her platinum hair was a mare's nest of burst and tangled up spider legs and guts.

The suitors had meanwhile all taken off their codpieces and stood over the twitching girl. Two of them looked quite bitten-up by the spiders, but clearly not enough to either incapacitate them or give them erectile dysfunction.

In a fight of bugs versus birds, the birds generally win, Hailey thought, in reference to the men's beaked plague masks.

After a game of rock-paper-scissors to determine who went first, a short and hairy man stepped forward, knelt between Jessica's splayed legs and slipped his manhood into her. When he encountered her hymen's resistance, he seemed to hang suspended in space and time for a moment, and then he was through it and into her most precious depths. Jessica merely jerked like stabbed meat. That was her sole reaction.

Hailey wondered if the older girl felt anger beneath her paralysis. *For certain, whatever fantasies, dreams or nightmares she entertained about tonight, none of them involved this scenario—herself laid out half-comatose in the middle of the road under harsh streetlights.*

"What the . . . ?"

Thinking that Annette had found her and was shooting arrows at her, Hailey leapt back as something streaked past her hair.

But it was just a drone, flying past her to get in close to the action. Once out in the street, the aerial machine zipped back up into the sky, and a moment later the image on the monitor across from Hailey switched to a view from directly above the mattress on which the short and hairy man was lustily thrusting away between Jessica's legs. The man thrust two or three more times, then stiffened and went limp on Jessica.

When he got to his feet, the drone overhead projected the image of Jessica's thighs and sex; a close-up of her labia looking as red as rose petals with a trickle of semen draining from between them.

Jessica seemed unaware that she'd just lost her virginity. She seemed lost somewhere else, a traveler through a world of paralytic pain that forbade the consideration of such minor mortal concerns as sexual morality. She twitched and shivered on the mat as if having a spontaneous orgasm . . . or as if dying.

Another game of rock-paper-scissors. Another man knelt between Jessica's thighs and began thrusting.

Hailey grimaced at what she was watching. *Okay, I should leave here right now.* But she didn't move from where she'd crouched.

It struck her then that there might be some subliminal message being projected to the audience of *The Virgin*, some grand statement about rape culture and the general objectification of women; something that only such a gratuitous display of sex and violence as this could convey to the watchers. She admitted to herself that she might be wrong about this though, and that the true reason might just be that the Hellers had a creepy sense of aesthetics.

But why else are the 'rest of the cast'—as it were—masked, and I and the other virgins alone unmasked, as if we're sacrifices being offered up on society's perverse altar?

Hailey wanted to get upset at what she was witnessing from just six yards off, but she knew that such a moral stance would be a hypocritical one.

Actually, she was very glad that Jessica had just been eliminated.

And, despite any appearances to the contrary, Jessica ISN'T being raped. She signed the same contract as all the rest of us girls. And the wording of that contract was very clear on what was required of us—'One act of coitus is permitted under any circumstances in which it may occur . . . the hymen must be ruptured . . . blah, blah, blah . . .'

Hailey didn't remember the rest, but the essence of it (explained in detail by Hi, Men's lawyers before she signed) was that whichever suitor overpowered a virgin in the contest was permitted to fuck her. Violently if necessary.

But only once. Once she was no longer a virgin, she was out of the competition and no one could touch her anymore.

(This was one reason for the heavy presence of guards on the show: to ensure that no suitors or virgins harassed deflowered girls. This might not be intentional—often contestants didn't realize that others had been eliminated.)

Of course, as Jessica's case now vividly demonstrated, if you got caught by more than one guy . . . well, you got gangbanged. Hailey winced as she watched the quartet of penetrations on the platinum blonde's jerking and quivering body, the tip of each penis dripping semen as its owner got back to his feet.

Damn, talk about making sure a hymen is destroyed for good, she thought in instinctive horror, her hand dropping to her own crotch, which felt disagreeably warm and juicy as if the sex acts she was watching were arousing her.

She had to admit though that there wasn't anything particularly violent about the sex. Jessica was in no condition to resist penetration, so the suitors weren't being nasty to her. Each of the four men just stepped up, knelt down, thrust and came in her and stepped away again, while their semen drained out of the trembling young woman on the mattress in thick streams.

Then, after once more fixing their mesh protectors back over their crotches, the four suitors high-fived each other for a job well done and then melted away into the night looking for another virgin to deflower.

Thankfully they didn't come Hailey's way.

***

Once the four suitors had left the street, Hailey heard the sound of an approaching motor.

Finally, she thought as the white ambulance rode up the street and parked beside the twitching girl on the mattress.

The medics alighted from the rear of the ambulance. After a quick examination by one of them, Jessica was strapped down to a gurney and lifted up into the ambulance.

The medics got back in. The white vehicle reversed, backed into the first driveway it reached and then drove out again and headed down the street.

The mattress remained there, with that tiny splash of blood in its middle like an invitation to come disvirgin someone else there.

Hailey wasn't impressed by the trickle that Jessica had bled; she was downright disappointed that there wasn't more blood. Four guys and that's all there is? She'd always imagined that virgins bled like the metaphorical pigs.

As shown on the monitor opposite Hailey, the overhead drone zoomed in for a close-up of the mattress, then it looped around and flew off past her again.

The white ambulance turned the street corner and vanished from sight.

Bye, girl, Hailey thought after it. *Have a pleasant trip back home to daddy!*

Then, still not realizing that all this while she'd been standing beside one of the four chapels, Hailey turned and headed for the top of the street.

Her logic was simple enough: *Those bird-headed guys all went THAT way, so I'm going THIS way.*

But just as she was about to cross the road again to return to the cafeteria, Hailey caught sight of a telltale flash of red hair coming around the side of the cafeteria building.

"Fuck!" she gasped aloud as her eyes locked with those of Rhianna Jackson.

The black girl smiled at Hailey. Then she raised her axes and, accelerating like she was representing the USA in the hundred meters dash at the Olympics, charged across the street at Hailey.

"You're mine, bitch!" she thundered as she closed the distance between them.

Rhianna might have been fast, but panic and terror gave Hailey wings. Hell no, Hailey wasn't hanging around to face Rhianna, who at the moment looked like she ate nice girls like Hailey for breakfast.

I'd rather deal with mad Annette and her arrows, she thought while dashing helter-skelter between the buildings in an attempt to escape Rhianna, and without any consideration of where she was headed.

CHAPTER 15

Rhianna

"Dammit! She got away!"

Rhianna kicked a tree when she realized that Hailey had escaped her. Then, realizing that her actions might give her position away, she calmed down and slipped through a doorway to regroup.

She found herself inside some sort of carpenter's workshop. The room contained three sturdy workbenches and a good number of open cabinets that held trays of nails and screws of various sizes. Cut lumber was propped up against the far wall. Shelves and racks on the other walls held tools—hammers, saws, smoothing planes and rolls of sandpaper, tape rules and straightedges, and lots of other stuff that she didn't recognize.

She sat on a high stool, placed both axes on her dusky thighs, and began thinking.

I've gotta get rid of that bitch Annette! This is the second time tonight that she's almost killed me! When the show began I thought Trailer Trash Princess was the one to watch out for, but now I know better!

Rhianna examined a cut on her left thigh—a weeping red groove through brown skin—where an arrow had grazed her.

She wasn't scared. She felt thrilled, exhilarated to once more be on the hunt. She felt impatient; she wanted to begin sniffing Hailey out. But Rhianna was a very cautious young woman—growing up in her hard-knock neighborhood with all the druggies and would-be pimps, you had to have street smarts—and she felt this was a good time to put things in perspective; to ditch Plan A if it wasn't working and switch to Plan B instead.

So she thought: *I know Hailey's around here somewhere. Girl can't have run that far, she's gotta still be nearby. So how 'bout if I forget Annette for the time being and work on taking Hailey out of the equation instead? That li'l mouse'll be easy to neutralize. And I also gotta remember those two guys I almost bumped into a short while ago. Gotta evade them while sniffing Hailey out.*

***

This time last year, Rhianna Oprah Jackson had been just another poor black girl from Chicago's inner city who was desperate to break out of the cycle of poverty her family had lived in since the turbulent days of the civil rights movement.

She'd been working in a diner, where her job consisted of washing dishes, cleaning the floor and taking out the garbage. It was a job that paid bottom dollar and had no career advancement prospects whatsoever.

Rhianna had thought it absurd that someone was willing to pay her ten million dollars to keep what she was merely days away from presenting free of charge to her boyfriend Lamont as her birthday gift on his 21st birthday.

That, of course, was before she discovered her talent for violent behavior. She'd found being able to take out her anger on whoever pissed her off without any fear of the police getting involved both liberating and exhilarating.

Scruples and ethics out of the way, Rhianna Oprah Jackson had hacked and slashed her way to victory.

And afterwards she'd loved being rich. Hi, Men! had paid out her winnings under the camouflage of an online lottery, so she'd had no problems explaining her sudden wealth either to her parents or the IRS. She'd bought her father and mother a new house and a Mercedes, put a million dollars in their bank account, and then looked around for how to invest the rest of her money. Rhianna loved music and wanted to own her own Hip Hop record label.

It was while basking in the glory of winning *The Virgin* last year that she'd gotten the email from Hi, Men! asking if she'd be interested in competing again.

She'd immediately replied in the affirmative. Oh yes, she'd *love* to relive the experience and win more money.

It wasn't that she wanted to murder anyone—she wasn't bloodthirsty in real life; was humble and well-behaved. She just wanted another chance to fight without rules.

In a sense she saw *The Virgin* as the ultimate catfight scene. Girl-on-girl violence with no boundaries.

That girl—Melanie—whom she'd beheaded during last year's final fight? That hadn't been premeditated, it had happened on the spur of the moment. She'd felt a red haze fill her brain and seemingly time-warp her back to the Stone Age, to a cavewoman level of reasoning in which survival at any cost was all that mattered.

2 million years BC—*she* was the human in distress and Melanie Barker was the saber-toothed tiger.

What happened next had been the product of pure atavistic instinct. By the time she regained her senses, she'd been holding up Melanie's head for the cameras.

But premeditated or not, that moment *had* felt totally fucking awesome though. She wouldn't mind feeling like that again. In fact, she was looking forward to doing so.

Rhianna's resolution to keep her virginity for one more year had of course meant she'd had to find another sexual present for Lamont's birthday. But she'd worked that out okay—he'd been delighted with what she'd given him. (At the moment Lamont thought she was attending a Baptist girl's retreat at her Uncle Tom's church down south in Dallas.)

And yes, despite her new wealth, Rhianna and Lamont were still dating. She really, utterly, truly loved him. She'd promised him her virginity as her gift for his birthday this year, which was in a week's time. Assuming her hymen survived this competition. But that was almost a given. Rhianna didn't consider any of the other girls as valid competition, not even the trailer trash princess Teresa. Sure the girl looked tough, but she was certain to crumble under the show's pressure.

The only virgin that Rhianna had been unsure of was that old witch Annette. There was just something in Annette's eyes that unsettled Rhianna each time she looked at her.

***

Now, Rhianna stepped out of the house and resumed her hunt.
Alright, Hailey, which house are you in?
Conscious of the unseen eyes watching her, she moved to the next house and peeked into its windows. She now made a point of keeping

a wall behind her at all times. That way Annette couldn't shoot at her. She'd also no longer stroll down a street like she owned it; doing so was asking for an arrow in the face.

She saw no one though this house's windows and heard no sounds either, so she padded quietly on to the next in line. No luck there too, so after looking left, right and left again as if expecting traffic, she dashed across the road and pressed herself against the side of a front porch.

The damp bricks made her shiver. She hoped it wouldn't rain tonight like it had on last year's show. Sure this bikini getup made the girls look sexy, but once you got drenched, it was chill-ville from then on.

Hey, what's that? Or rather, who is that? A shadow had flickered across a window on the other side of the street. *Is that Hailey . . . or Annette?*

The shadow came again. A silhouette of fingers touched the sill and vanished.

Someone's hiding over there. Then Rhianna's lips creased in a suspicious frown. *Or, should that rather be 'something' is hiding there? Mr. and Mrs. Heller have a sick sense of humor, that's for sure, with all those crazy booby traps they've got set up around the game zone.*

***

Rhianna had personal experience of the booby traps. Last year, she'd tracked a wounded suitor into a cafeteria. The man had wanted a place where he could bandage his wounded forearm; he hadn't known Rhianna was right behind him. She followed him inside and ducked behind the counter, intending to hack his other arm open to eliminate him.

But then the suitor had walked over to get something from the freezer at the far end of the room. This was a huge freezer—with double doors.

Because of the pain he was in, the suitor wasn't paying attention to his surroundings. Rhianna was though, and she saw the almost invisible tripwire on the floor.

She'd have called out a warning to the man, but he'd already stepped on the wire. And next . . .

No sooner had the suitor touched the freezer than it slid completely aside to reveal a wide recess behind it in which lurked a giant grizzly bear.

The grizzly was clearly mad at being cooped in that tiny space for so long, and what happened next was a horrifying mess that made Rhianna throw up. The bear tore the suitor to pieces, ripped him up like he was made of red Styrofoam and tomato catsup. The fact that the man had a bird mask on must have made the bear think it was dealing with some uppity raven or stork.

Rhianna had gotten out of there in a hurry. As she'd run off she'd seen security arrive with nets to subdue the grizzly so it didn't escape into the rest of the game zone.

***

So this year, Rhianna was very wary of shadows behind windows. They could be anything—mountain lions, chimps, wolves, giant boa constrictors that could swallow you whole, gators or cayman, literally anything dangerous.

No one ever said it'd be easy to win ten million bucks, she thought, flexing her fingers around the grip of her axes. *The Hellers don't own a money tree and they aren't Santa Claus either. So I need eyes in the back of my head tonight.*

She glanced down at her watch and noted that it was now twenty minutes into the second period. She shrugged and looked back up at the window across the street. Other than for time, she didn't pay attention to the wristwatch—she saw no point in asking it for directions.

To Rhianna's mind, everyone in the game zone was lost, no matter where they were. *We're trapped in a circle and going round in circles. What else d'you need to know?*

The fingers across the road parted the window drapes. She caught a flash of a head, but whose damn head was it? Then the fingers parted the drapes some more.

She decided it had to be Hailey over there. *That girl is just a scaredy-cat, nothing more.* Besides, Rhianna was certain Trailer Trash Princess wouldn't hide like that. *She's too much like me—a born fighter.*

And as for Annette . . . Rhianna scowled at the arrow-wound on her thigh. *Just wait till I get my hands on that old witch. Oh, I'll teach her to shoot at me!*

Holding her pair of axes at the ready, Rhianna made her way back across the road and then slowly crept towards the house with the silhouettes. She did her best to blend in with the walls. Her target house faced open space; at any instant an arrow could come streaking at her.

But no arrows came flying at her and she made it to the building alive.

Unwilling to stand outside tempting danger, she opened the front door and entered the house.

"Hi, baby, I've been wondering when you'd stop being shy and come in to say hi!"

Damn, it's a trap. Before she could back out of the door again, the suitor had slammed it shut behind her. He was still standing by the window, but he'd rigged up a mechanism to shut the door, a wooden pole that now slotted itself behind the door handle, meaning Rhianna was locked inside here with him.

So she faced him instead. He was taller than her, but this was normal enough—she was just five feet three inches tall—most guys were taller than she was.

He was unarmed, his knife lying on the sill near his fingers, so she charged him, axes swinging. She was a fighter and this was a fight, so she went all out for it.

But he anticipated her coming and got out of her way and grabbed her wrists.

Then he swung her around so she was pressed flat against the wall, and cranked her right hand up behind her back until her arm felt about to break. Now she cursed herself for not taking any self-defense classes over the last year. It wasn't really her fault though. She'd been paid a million dollars to keep her virginity intact and she wasn't about to do any hard exercising that might put the precious and delicate moneymaking tissue between her legs in jeopardy. (Rhianna had been a track-and-field star in high school and she considered it one of God's bona fide miracles that her hymen had survived all those relay races she'd run and all the long-jumping she'd done. Those should have shredded it for sure.)

"Drop the axes, baby," the suitor grunted, his codpiece pressing hard against her bare buttocks. "Both of 'em, or I'll pop your arm like I'm tearing off a chicken wing."

She dropped the axes. Hearing them clatter down by her feet felt like flushing ten million dollars down the toilet.

I should've known it was a damn trick!

Once she'd let go of the axes, he let go of her arm and gripped her neck instead. However, this was worse for her, not better. She realized that he was choking her. Soon she began feeling lightheaded. She tried to turn around and kick at him but he pressed her harder against the wall, till her breasts ground painfully against the wooden boards. He also wedged a knee between her thighs, pinning her in place.

"Fight and I'll hurt you," he said, his voice thick with sexual excitement.

She nodded quickly and the choking feeling reduced a little.

He popped the catches of his codpiece and discarded it to one side. She winced on feeling his stiff manhood prod her buttocks. The loss of money that this penis represented really hurt her. She felt like she was facing a firing squad.

"Baby, you're the first black girl I've been with since my sister's bestie Latasha ditched me in high school for that basketball player."

She believed him. He sounded young too, early twenties like.

He yanked her G-string off, then roughly kicked her sneakers apart. She tried to force her feet back together, but he choked her again till she quit struggling. "Uh uh, that isn't happening. Best you just relax and endure it, baby."

"Hey, man, how 'bout if you and I make a deal? I'll suck you off now and then we'll work together to eliminate all the competition. Think about it, huh? That way we'll keep all the prize money to ourselves."

He paused, considering her words, then replied, "No deal, baby. I'd rather deal with a rattlesnake. I saw all that footage of you from last year. I'm not gonna let you stab me in the back like that."

He still had that choking grip on her throat and she felt close to passing out. Blood was thundering in her ears. Additionally, the long beak of his mask pressed painfully against her right ear. She heard him spit on his other hand and then felt him rub the spit on his penis. He spit again and lubricated her labia with it. She felt the fatness of his manhood between her legs, felt him crouch and position himself and then pull her right buttock to the side.

Rhianna thought desperately. *No no no no no! What can I do? There's only one thing I can do now.*

"Get ready, baby, 'cos here I come!"

"Oh, so you're going old-school on me?"

She jerked her hips forward at the exact moment he thrust into her, and also got a hand down to cover her vagina. She timed it perfectly and he slipped into her anus instead. She felt a fullness in her backside and realized that she'd accomplished her aim.

Her suitor, however, didn't seem to realize that he'd missed his aim. Or maybe he was just so relieved to finally be inside a woman's body tonight that he didn't care? Because she was certain it had to be agony walking around for hours with an erection and no one to stick it into. Lamont got cranky if she even made him wait twenty minutes till a movie ended before coming to bed. And this suitor seemed to be about Lamont's age.

Whichever was the case, the man showed no sign of noticing or caring that he was in the wrong female hole.

"Oh shit, baby!" he gasped in delight, his muscular torso pressing hard against her so she felt compressed between two walls. "Yeah, I knew you'd be a good one for me. Now just relax and take this first-ever nut that I'm about to pump inside you and hope you don't get preggered up from it."

He humped away at her, his muscular hands first raising her up onto her toes so he could get deep inside her, and then almost lifting her completely off her feet as he crushed her against the wall.

Rhianna tried to relax but couldn't. To her chagrin and embarrassment, the familiar sensations in her backside were producing familiar results in her vagina. The hand she'd slid between her legs wasn't helping matters either.

The thing was, that instead of giving Lamont her girly parts as his birthday gift last year, she'd given him her ass instead (she'd been a virgin there too), and that's how they'd been doing it for the past year. That and oral.

Being sexually aroused and yet wanting to remain a virgin was a familiar feeling for Rhianna. She often wondered how she'd survived an additional full year of yearning to be penetrated the right way. Alright, the million dollars had helped a lot.

And now, as the suitor thrust into her behind, it felt as if all the night's tension was rushing down to her crotch. She was suddenly very aroused; excited well beyond her ability to control her reactions and remain objective about her objectives. And there was also the choking going on; so maybe she wasn't quite right in the head at the moment.

As he pumped her, she rubbed her clitoris and before she knew it she was coming.

"Oh, don't stop, baby! Don't stop!"

She felt very silly gasping out these words. Then her orgasm was over and the man behind her was slowing his own thrusts as his own climax overcame him.

"ShiiiiiiTTT!" he groaned, squeezing Rhianna's neck so hard that she almost passed out from the pain. Then he filled up her butt with semen.

He slipped out of her and let go of her neck. Her legs were trembling too much to hold her upright, so she slid to the floor and let the semen run out of her ass.

The bird-masked man staggered back and sat in a chair. He was still hard from the boner pills.

He laughed. "Now that wasn't too bad, was it, baby? Two hundred grand for me and none for you."

Rhianna smirked at him. "That's what you think, motherfucker." Now that he was no longer choking her, her mind had quickly cleared up. Also, rather than weaken her, her orgasm had empowered her. "Man, I'm still a virgin where it counts."

"Huh?" At first he didn't understand her amusement. But she was sitting against the wall with her legs parted wide and he quickly realized that his semen was leaking from her ass and not her vagina. Her anus seemed well-used—a little slack even—but her labia looked as close together as if nothing had ever parted them.

His eyes widened and he stared down at his erection. "Oh, you dirty, dirty bitch!"

She giggled. "Oh, man, I hope I didn't shit on your dick now, did I?"

"Shit! You tricked me!"

She scowled at him. "Motherfucker, how's it *my* fault if *you* can't tell the difference between ass and pussy, huh?"

"Well, I can easily fix that!" Enraged by her 'deceit,' he leapt up from his chair and hurried towards her.

She watched him come. This time she was ready for him. As he bent down to grab her, she moved out of his way, rolling to her left. Before he could straighten up again she snatched one of her axes off the floor and, crouching low, slammed the blade of the axe into the back of his right ankle.

With a loud popping sound, his right Achilles tendon was severed. Rhianna had rammed the axe in so hard that it had wedged itself in the suitor's ankle bones. She had to jerk it hard to get it out again.

The axe blade came free with a gush of blood just as the suitor realized what had happened. With a scream of pain, he turned to grab Rhianna but she'd already scooted away from him across the floor. He took a step towards her and his right leg twisted beneath him and he went down in a heap.

She laughed at him as he sat there, gripping his bleeding, crippled ankle. "It sure don't look like you'll be cashing in on my cherry now, does it, motherfucker?"

"Fuck you, you dirty whore!"

"I oughta bury this axe in your head for calling me a whore," she said. "But you just made me come, so I'm gonna let you live."

And besides, he'd taught her something: this 'choking during sex' thing. Though she'd read about it online, she'd never tried it before. She was going to try it out with Lamont to see if it produced the same exhilarating sense of almost dying during orgasm. But maybe it wouldn't, that might just have happened because she was so wired up from the show.

Or maybe because this guy actually was killing me.

Giggling uncontrollably, she pointed to the suitor's crotch. "Hey, your dick's still hard. You some kind of masochist, or what?" Then she burst out laughing.

The suitor was still gasping out insults at her when, white G-string now back in place and clutching her two axes again, Rhianna left the house.

CHAPTER 16

Annette

About a minute after Rhianna walked out of the building, Annette Morrison strode in through its front door.

She looked around the front room and saw the wounded suitor sitting on a chair. "Hey, there!"

"The black girl went that way," the suitor said without much interest, pointing left to indicate where Rhianna had headed to after crippling him. He had one hand clamped around his right ankle, which he was trying to tourniquet with a length of curtain cord. He'd removed his mask and was young and quite cute, with dark hair and a mustache. "Just head left," he added. "You'll catch her if you hurry."

Annette smiled at him. "I know," she said in a voice laden with cruelty. "I'm actually here to see you." That said, she quickly notched an arrow to her bow and aimed it at him.

"Hey, lady, what's the matter with you?" the suitor pleaded, seeing the sadistic smile on Annette's face. "You can see that I'm wounded. I ain't a threat to your virginity anymore."

Annette pouted a kiss at him. "Oh yes, you are a threat to me, honey. You've still got a boner."

"What? But . . . Ah—!" the man's mouth gaped open to protest.

Annette let fly with the arrow, which hit the man in his open mouth, slit his tongue in two, shattered his neck vertebrae and cut through his spinal cord, and then finally pinned his head to the plasterboard wall behind him.

"*Now* you aren't a threat to me," Annette said with glee. She strode over to the dead man and felt his biceps. "In fact, kid, I really, really like you in this condition."

That said, she put down her bow and walked over to the window to pick up the dead man's knife.

She stared out of the window for a few moments, feeling very pleased with her accomplishments so far tonight.

Oh, but there's more to do, so much more. Annette intended to leave her bloody mark on this *Virgin* competition.

A cold smile on her lips, her green eyes glittering, she turned away from the window.

She returned to the dead suitor, stabbed the knife into his belly and began slicing upward.

CHAPTER 17

Teresa

Hell, I don't get this. Now where the hell has everyone vanished to? Half an hour ago they were coming at me out of the walls, and now the game zone is like a cemetery. It can't be that the guys are all avoiding me now, can it? Hey, guys, I'm not Annette! Which makes me wonder—where is Annette? One moment she's shooting at me and the next I can't find her either. Lucky for the biatch that I can't though, 'cos once I lay my hands on her, I'll wring her neck like a chicken's!

But, hey, this is really strange. I've been walking around for ten minutes and . . . even the drones seem to be avoiding me. This is so creepy that I wish Annette would shoot an arrow at me just so I'll know I'm not alone out here.

And . . . hey, where the hell am I anyway? Time to tap for map! Hey, magic wristwatch map, where am I? Lemme see: I'm halfway up Third Street and . . . so, this is me here and . . . that blue dot across the road from me means . . . that's a chapel over there! It's behind those two houses and through the park. Okay, I'll go have a rest in there for the next quarter-hour. Maybe by then all the vanished folks will have reappeared. Also, I need to pee anyway and I'm not crazy enough to squat out here with all the crazies about.

And for fuck's sake—will someone please hand me the keys to these goddamned handcuffs!? The chain keeps rattling against the axe blade like a bell announcing my presence in the neighborhood!

CHAPTER 18

Hailey

Only when Hailey was too exhausted to keep running did she stop. Then she hid beneath a solitary tree to catch her breath.

She watched and listened. Listened for Rhianna's approach. But she both saw and heard no one. Even the bugs were silent out here, as if they'd either been fumigated out of the game zone altogether or all been caught and packed into cages and boxes to be used in Miriam Heller's booby traps.

The silence was very spooky. *Never visited a ghost town before, but this one can't be far off the mark.*

A chill wind began blowing and she took this as her signal to resume moving. She looked up. The night sky was as black as crow feathers; there was still no moon in sight. But all the lights in the nearby houses were on.

Oh, genie of the watch on my wrist, where am I? She shifted her knife from right hand to left and tapped the watch on.

She was right at the top of the game zone. A few steps forward and she was looking out at the point where the five main roads converged, the peak of the 'A' as it were. A wide expanse of concrete flooring like a factory parking lot and illuminated by a dozen streetlights. The concrete floor blended into the main road that encircled the game zone, and around that ran the zone's 10-foot-high brick wall.

She frowned at the brick wall. *Too late to escape now.* Not that she would if she could anyway. She'd made up her mind to tough this thing out; to survive for as long as she could in the game. *If I lose the money, it won't be for want of trying.*

On the opposite side of this wide-open space stood the mall. That's what the watch map called it, though Hailey thought it actually looked more like part of an administrative complex. The mall was a two-story building which, as she crossed the road conjunction towards it, she discovered was actually semi-circular in design, with both floors given over to shops, those on the upper floor being accessed by an exterior balcony. Downstairs there was a coffee shop, a candy shop, a jeweler's, a barbershop and such like. The odd one out was the taxidermy shop with its display of stuffed deer, beavers and raccoons. Upstairs one sign proclaimed 'Sports Goods,' while another read 'Liquor Store'; and there was also a bridal store and a nail salon. And she'd only read those signs on the side she was approaching from.

Welcome to the small mall, she thought.

With nowhere else to go for the moment, she decided to enter the mall, realizing for the first time that in her mad rush to escape Rhianna, she'd run across two main streets, and had now (at least in a manner of speaking) just crossed back over them again.

Once she'd confirmed, by peeking into the coffee shop, that this mall building was an actual building and not one of the fake framework houses that filled the game zone, she walked around to its front entrance, with her intent being to climb the stairs and explore the Sports Goods shop for something to augment her puny armory of a single knife. She tried to remember if sports shops sold hunting rifles or not. At least she should find a baseball bat in there; hopefully one of those aluminum ones.

But once Hailey stepped through the building's marble archway, she heard voices.

With the mall's semicircular design, its interior was built in two sections. The outer section where she stood formed a concrete loop of interior and exterior shops, then there was a similarly looped driveway space that was about twenty feet wide; and then on the other side of the curved driveway and also built in semicircular shape, stood a small cinema hall, the top floor of which housed a McDonald's.

One of the giant monitors hung right over Hailey, its screen on standby—a reminder of the omnipresence of Hi, Men's CCTV surveillance.

Hailey froze and listened. The voices came again and now she tried to isolate their source. Her first thought was that they were coming from the separate building opposite her, but the McDonald's' lights were all off and the doors to the movie hall were chained and padlocked together.

They're on my right . . . near the end of the mall.

She set off that way, conscious that she was being quite stupid. *The sensible thing to do is leave and look for the chapel that my watch tells me is down No. 1 Street. But . . .*

But she was tired of running. *The girls I'm fleeing from are no different from myself—mere flesh and blood, with breasts and butts and unused pussies exactly like mine. Okay, so the guys are bigger but . . . screw that, it's time to start fighting.*

So she cautiously neared the voices. The last three rooms on the right were of the 'fake' kind—framework structures containing packing boxes. A quick look around the mall explained why this wooden construction was necessary. Apparently the right end of the building had at some point collapsed and had needed to be rebuilt in a hurry. A look across the game zone's encircling road, at the large pile of removed masonry dumped against the zone's exterior brick wall, supported this theory.

For a moment, Hailey toyed with the idea of escape. The piled masonry would make the wall easy to scale. All she had to do was sneak past the last room where the conversation was taking place, cross the road, and she'd be out of here in five minutes.

But what if Miriam's got quicksand or a moat with gators on the other side of the wall? Or a guard patrol who'll simply toss me back over it? What then?

And besides, she was already hooked. She wanted to know what was being discussed in that last room, because she'd already recognized one of the speakers as Rhianna Jackson. Rhianna, she of the dusky skin and fiery red hair.

What the hell is she doing up here?

There was only one way to find out. Hailey slipped into the third-to-last room and eavesdropped by the interconnecting door (these three 'fake house' rooms were linked by wide doorways). She winced as the wooden floor creaked. The floor looked older than the walls, like it was part of the original building. Hailey made a note to avoid the parts of the floor that looked rotted. It would be easy to slip through and break a leg. Thankfully, however, there were no tripwires in evidence in here.

She settled down and listened. This place was so out of the way that Rhianna was making no attempt to be quiet. She clearly didn't expect anyone else to come to the mall tonight.

Now this is interesting.

There were two suitors with the black girl, one of whom Hailey recognized. Not facially of course, as he still had his bird mask in place, but she knew him because his right thigh was bandaged with bloodstained fabric. This was clearly the man she'd earlier stabbed. He hadn't spoken yet but she was certain of it.

Rhianna and the two suitors were sitting on crates and she was waving an axe at them to emphasize her words. The axe was bloodstained like she'd been in a fight.

"Alright," she was saying in a relaxed voice, "so that's the deal I'm proposing. You help me, and you each get a million dollars."

"What's the guarantee?" the man Hailey had stabbed asked. (She instantly recognized his voice.)

Rhianna smiled. "You got my word on it."

The other man said, "You could change your mind afterwards."

Rhianna rolled her eyes. "No I won't. I really wonder why no one trusts me. When not competing here, I'm a very well behaved young woman. My father's the organist for a Baptist church and my mom sings in the choir." Then she shrugged. "Oh, alright. Let's do it like this." She looked from man to man. "You guys agree that the Hellers are recording everything we do and say, even out here, right?" She pointed out through a window and waved at a drone that was zipping by, then looked in at them again. "Well, do you?"

Both men slowly nodded, once again making that weird motion like chickens pecking up corn.

"So, it's simple then," Rhianna said. "They'll be watching and recording this too." She got to her feet and waved her hands about. "Hey, Miriam, lip-read me! If I win, these guys each get a million dollars out of my cut!" She said it three more times, each time turning to face a different corner of the room while speaking, then turned back to the two bird-masked men. "Okay, so that's now on record. You guys trust me now?"

Hailey's suitor nodded. "I like the way you do business, girl."

"Yeah, me too," the other man agreed with a laugh. "So, alright, now how do we go about doing this?"

Rhianna mused on that for a moment. "See, what I'm thinking is . . . okay, at the moment there's just ten of us left in the competition— four girls and six of you guys." She tapped her axe against the crate she was sitting on. "Now, seeing that us three are working together now . . ." She paused and frowned. "Hey, are you two even listening to me? What's going on here?"

"Hey, can we seal the deal with a blowjob?" the second man asked. "You've got such pretty lips that my boner won't let me concentrate on what you're saying."

"Yeah, even a handjob would calm *me* down," Hailey's suitor agreed, tapping his mesh codpiece. "Dunno what was in those pills they gave us, but my cock feels like a stone. And for us, jacking off is strictly against the show's rules."

"Sorry, guys," Rhianna said coldly, "but we ain't got no time for that shit now." She checked her watch. We've just twenty minutes to second recess; gotta act fast."

"Aw, c'mon, girl. You can jack us both off at once; save time that way."

"No. I'll suck you both off during the recess period, how's that?"

"Why wait? Aw shit, man—wish I was nearby when they caught that platinum blonde; I'd have squirted some of this jizz off. But we were on the other size of the zone then and couldn't get over there in time to join the proceedings."

"Listen, guys," Rhianna explained patiently, "it ain't that I'm against sucking you both off, but blowjobs take time and I've only got one mouth. It might take me five minutes each to make you both come, and all that while we'll be wasting valuable competition time. So that's why I'm saying—wait till the recess. Then I can take my time to satisfy you both and I can assure you guys I'll be worth the wait." While speaking the black girl unconsciously spread her legs at such an angle that Hailey noticed she'd dyed her pubic hair red too.

The suitors grunted assent and Rhianna resumed speaking. "So where was I? Yeah, so there's just ten competitors left and with us three working together, that means we've seven people to take out."

"Who first?"

"The guys first, then we'll tackle the girls. I'm thinking to use myself as bait. I can lure the guys out here one at a time and you two can knock 'em out and tie 'em up. There's gotta be some rope and duct tape in the shops—"

"Knock the guys out? That's gonna be easier said than done with everyone armed and suspicious."

"Kill 'em then. Either way, it's gonna be two machetes or axes against one. Do whatever you have to do to take them out of the competition." She got up and grinned. "And then we'll hunt down the girls one at a time." She laughed loudly. "And . . . we'll certainly give the audience the show that they're paying for. Rejoice, guys—you two motherfuckers will get to deflower all three of the remaining virgins."

Hailey's suitor laughed. "Yeah, I'm looking forward to seeing that girl again—the hot blonde who stabbed me in the leg. When we catch her, I'm gonna do such a number on her cherry that she'll remember it . . . and me . . . for the rest of her life."

***

Hailey hadn't understood why, after winning last year's *Virgin* contest, Rhianna was back again this year. It seemed crazy, if one was already a millionairess, to expose oneself to such unnecessary danger again. But now, hearing the black girl calmly planning the death of her adversaries, and remembering the look on Rhianna's face when she'd been holding up that brunette's head . . . that joyous smirk like she'd accomplished some personal goal, Hailey felt she understood Rhianna.

She just likes hurting people and this underground show provides her with ample opportunity to do so.

Shivering, Hailey, resolved there and then to stay as far away from Rhianna Jackson as she possibly could.

Which is easier said than done, silly girl. 'Cos here I am standing right next to her and I walked in here by myself.

***

"The person I'm most worried about is Annette," Hailey's suitor said.

"Yeah, that bitch is a goddamn threat," the other man nervously agreed. "She's killed two guys already with those arrows of hers and there's no telling where she is at any point in time. Oh, man, did you see how she shot José, even though he was as good as useless? Shot him in the mouth when he was begging her to let him live! She's just a sadistic bi—"

"Forget Annette!" Rhianna said sharply. "She ain't nothin'. Leave her to me. I find her and I'll deal with her. You guys can count on that."

117

"If you say so," the second man said. "So you say we should just stay here?"

Rhianna nodded. "Yeah, just wait for me to return with the prey. They'll think they're hunting me down, not realizing that they're walking into our trap." Hailey's suitor got to his feet then and Rhianna asked, "Hey, where you going?"

"I gotta take a pee," the man replied, turning towards the door connecting the rooms. "Damn urine feels like it's making my damn cock even harder."

The other man laughed. "Hey, man, why not just step *outside* and pee?"

"Hell no! Not with the way Annette's been handling that bow. I don't want her turning me into a pincushion. I'll go use the restroom in the cafeteria back there."

"Okay," Rhianna said. "But I won't be here when you get back, so remember the plan, huh?"

The suitor waved his agreement to Rhianna and then walked towards the first interconnecting door.

Hailey ducked back behind the door before he saw her. She hadn't expected the man to come towards her and (since she expected Rhianna to shortly step outside onto the mall walkway) could now no longer escape the third room unseen. She was now faced with a difficult choice: She could either remain still and hope the suitor was too preoccupied with peeing to notice her as he hurried past, or she could attack him and increase the odds in her own favor. She tried not to think ahead to any fight with redheaded Rhianna.

Hearing the suitor's footsteps almost at her own door, Hailey chose the latter option. Oh, she was so tired of running. Suddenly she was spoiling for a fight, no matter how ill-advised it was. Besides, she'd already escaped this guy once, hadn't she?

He took two steps into the room and she leapt at him. Not expecting any danger, he'd left his weapons in the last room and as such was easy prey for her. Not that she realized this when she struck at him.

"What the . . . ?" he gasped as she came at him.

Hailey had aimed for the man's chest, but he instinctively raised his right arm to protect himself as he turned towards her and his bicep deflected her knife towards his neck instead.

Hailey was as surprised as the suitor when her knife went into his throat.

Her knife's blade went in deep, deep, deep, and then he was staggering backward away from her with blood squirting from his throat; and the knife handle strained against her fist and she spread her fingers and let it go. She gaped at the man as he sank to his knees and finally pulled the knife from his throat, which only let the blood out faster.

Oh my God, I killed it! Hailey was unable to shake the inane thoughts rushing through her mind as she watched him die, thoughts that, no, this wasn't a man that she'd killed, it was a bird and that she was a bad person now, because it was wrong to hurt animals and . . .

Gasping loudly, the man finally crumpled to the floor and lay there jerking while the blood pooled around his shoulders.

"What the fuck?"

Hailey had been so horrified by what she'd done that she'd made no attempt to get away. Now she realized her peril. The other suitor was coming in through the interconnecting door, and Rhianna, who'd already left the last room by its main door, was now standing in the entranceway to this room.

Rhianna had an axe in her hand and she looked madder than a lioness interrupted during sex.

"You damn spoilsport!" she growled at Hailey and sprang at her.

Careful to avoid a repeat of what had happened earlier in the show when she'd tried to surprise Jessica Fox and had instead gone skidding across the floor on spilled oil, Hailey leapt over the dead man and tried to scramble through the back window.

"Get her!" Rhianna yelled.

The suitor had already grabbed her and was turning her around to face him. Desperate, she kneed him in the codpiece, then howled in pain as her knee reminded her of how tough that flimsy-looking material actually was.

"Hold her down!" Rhianna said, rushing over. Hailey got a leg up and kicked Rhianna in the midriff. Next thing she knew, Rhianna was coming at her again with her axe raised. She ducked out of the way and the axe thunked into the left window jamb. Rhianna tried to remove the axe, found it stuck, and took to punching Hailey instead.

The suitor was holding both of Hailey's hands clamped by her sides and all she kept seeing was a small black fist with purple fingernails coming up and hitting her in the jaw over and over again, rocking her head back and forth.

"Take this, you murdering bitch! And this!"

Thankfully, Rhianna wasn't much of a boxer and her punches lacked force, but at least one of them cut open Hailey's upper lip. And in addition, the young negress was jumping up and down in rage at the same time and that was having an effect on the wooden floor, which Hailey now remembered had rotten patches.

And I think we're standing right on one of them! she thought as the floor suddenly broke open and all three of them fell through it into the darkness below.

CHAPTER 19

Teresa

Since leaving the chapel where she'd holed up for a while, Teresa had been stalking a suitor who was holding a set of handcuffs.

Her reasoning was simple enough: he might have a key to the handcuffs on him, and she intended to jump him and take the key from him. Then she'd injure him badly enough to remove him from the show. If he fought her she might even hack his head off.

But getting the handcuffs off of her right wrist was the main reason she was following him. She hated the way the damned cuffs made her feel like an escaped convict. Being cuffed smacked too much of her following in her deadbeat family's footsteps again, as both of her father's brothers and one of her cousins were currently serving jail sentences for offences ranging from statutory rape to arson to armed robbery.

The man Teresa was following was several houses ahead, near a cafeteria, and didn't seem to suspect that she was behind him.

Then a monitor up ahead flickered on and she padded forward to see what it was showing. The suitor kept walking, he had already passed the monitor and didn't realize it had come on.

She watched a floor cave in and swallow the fighting Hailey, Rhianna, and a bird-masked suitor.

Wow! She stood in the shadows watching the digital screen, expecting someone to emerge alive from the hole. But no one did. After a few seconds the screen went back to standby mode, showing first a rainbow of color bars and then just the time.

Teresa felt intense fear. *Oh God, was that a booby-trap? Are they all dead now?*

Then she looked down the street and cursed. While she'd been watching TV, the suitor she'd been stalking had vanished.

CHAPTER 20

Hailey & Rhianna . . . Underground

Darkness and a jagged blotch of light overhead.

At first Hailey thought they'd triggered one of the booby-traps, but then she remembered that she'd not seen any tripwires in the room above. So it had just been the eroded floor caving in under them. That was some relief, but not much.

Because she was still in danger. Rhianna was groaning in pain on her left and Hailey had landed on the suitor, who was now sitting up and shoving her to one side of him. She rolled off him and squatted.

She looked around. The room was small, empty and dusty, with a bookshelf along one wall. A cabinet opposite the bookshelf carried a number of half-filled bottles. Ancient shattered planks lay piled in a corner as if this wasn't the first time the ceiling had caved in.

"Ouch! What just happened?" Rhianna asked, getting to her feet. Then she forgot her aches and looked around. "What the hell is this place?"

"Looks like we've fallen into the mall basement," the suitor replied, also getting to his feet.

The man had let go of Hailey, but she remained where she was. She realistically saw nowhere to run to. This room they were in had a partly open door but where it led was anyone's guess.

"We'll need something to stand on to get out of here," the suitor said, staring up at the hole above them. "A table preferably. Best of course would be a ladder, but failing that we'll need both a table and a chair. A table will easily let me get out, but I wouldn't trust the floor not to fall in again while I'm pulling you girls out."

"Maybe there's a way out," Rhianna said and pointed to the door. "That leads somewhere. And if this is a basement, it has to have an access door." She nodded at the suitor, then pointed down at Hailey.

"Hold on to her; she might try to run off somewhere down here."
Then she smiled at the man. "And our earlier deal just got an upgrade:
you can have the dead guy's share too. That's *two* million for you if I
win this damn show."

"Oh yeah!" The man pulled Hailey to her feet. "You heard the lady,
lady. Time to get a move on."

Hailey went willing, without a fuss. She was relieved that Rhianna
seemed to have forgotten her anger now. Up above, the black girl had
seemed intent on killing her for upsetting her plans.

Rhianna opened the door and they stepped out of the basement
room.

They emerged into a long underground corridor. The room they'd
exited was positioned about a third of the way along the corridor's
length, about a hundred feet away from its nearer end, which was
sealed off by a steel door. The corridor was lit by a series of overhead
lights set fifty feet apart. All the lights were on and they could see
down to the corridor's farther end, which ended at a second door, this
one slightly ajar and spilling out light. The corridor had several other
doors opening into it and also what looked like a side tunnel branching
off halfway to the open far-off door.

"You know, I don't think this is a basement," the suitor said in an
uneasy voice. "Well, not a normal one anyway."

Rhianna nodded. "I think you're right. Except if the mall once had
an underground level and the Hellers blocked it off when they bought
or hired this place." Her voice was confident, unworried. She looked
up and grinned at a large painting on the ceiling, a beautifully rendered
depiction of a bright red octopus. "Oh man, that's so cute—maybe
we're in the seafood section."

Rhianna looked down again and pointed to Hailey. "Dude, hold on
to her while I see if that steel door is unlocked."

The suitor took a firm grip on Hailey's left wrist. It felt like being
handcuffed to him. She watched Rhianna walk to the steel door at the
nearer end of the corridor, try turning its handle, and then turn around
to shake her head at them. "Nothing doing." Then she walked back
to them, pausing to try opening the two side doors along the way.
"And these are locked as well, and there's another cute octopus
painted on this one."

She rejoined them. "Let's head the other way. One of the other doors might be unlocked, or that open door at the end may even lead to a stairway."

"Which is certain to be blocked too," Hailey blurted out.

Rhianna stared narrowly at her. "Did you say something, bitch?"

Hailey couldn't be certain of her sense of direction, but she had the uncanny sense that the far end of this corridor actually extended outside of the game zone. And that was problematic because it meant that the show's organizers most likely didn't know of its existence. Also, down here, her wristwatch wouldn't give her any information except the time. And unlike Rhianna, she didn't think that the red octopus painted on the ceiling meant this was the seafood section. She didn't think it was cute either—it looked like something that wanted to eat them.

Leaving out the part about the octopus, she told Rhianna her suspicions. "I don't think exploring down here is good idea," she finished. "Haven't you noticed that this corridor isn't dusty? It's clean, which means it's still in use, and whoever uses it might be down here at the moment."

"Good for us," the suitor said, tightening his grip on her wrist till it felt like he was trying to break it. "The guy can show us the way out. And then"—the bird mask leaned in close as he spoke the next words with relish evident in his voice—"you're gonna lose your cherry, honey."

"Yeah, whatever," Hailey agreed, already resigned to the inevitable and simply praying it wouldn't hurt too badly when he penetrated her. "But, listen, Rhianna—don't you guys smell anything weird?"

Rhianna shrugged. "Nothing weird about the smell. Just disinfectant. Smells like a hospital."

"But under a mall? What would a hospital be doing underneath a mall? And a fake mall at that."

"Hmm," the suitor agreed, losing some of his cockiness as her nervousness infected him. "She's got a point, Rhianna. This ain't a good setup down here."

"Don't you start getting scared too," Rhianna retorted, starting off towards the open door at the corridor's end. "Just bring her along. There has to be a logical explanation for this place. And besides, we aren't loitering—we've got a good explanation for our being down here."

The suitor shoved Hailey ahead of him. "She's right, girl. Keep moving."

"We're unarmed," Hailey protested, pointing out the obvious. Her own knife lay upstairs in a pool of the dead suitor's blood; the living suitor had left his own weapons in the last room; and Rhianna's axe was still stuck in the window frame of the room they'd fallen from.

Rhianna turned from trying another locked side-door. "Will you please frigging shut up? We're not down here to fight anyone. All the fighting's happening upstairs."

"Alright," Hailey agreed as they went on. Her attention became focused on that door up ahead, the open one with its lights on. The room beyond it seemed to be waiting for them. She suspected that every other door along this corridor would prove to be locked, and that even the turnoff wouldn't lead anywhere. Almost as if fate was herding them to a specific, unpleasant destiny.

The side tunnel led to a metal grille beyond which stood a solid stone wall.

"Looks like the only way in or out of this place is that locked door behind us," the suitor said when Rhianna returned from checking the tunnel out. "I suggest that we just look in that last room for a table or ladder and get out of here."

Rhianna nodded. "Yeah, this place has begun giving me the creeps too. I keep thinking I can hear fish splashing somewhere nearby."

Hailey kept quiet. She'd heard the sounds too, like they were near a swimming pool; and the sounds were coming from that last room— the one that they seemingly had no choice now but to enter.

They reached the half-open door. Before Rhianna pushed it completely open Hailey saw that this door also had a red octopus drawn on it. Then Rhianna stepped inside the room and the suitor shoved Hailey in after her.

"Oh shit!" Rhianna instantly gasped.

The suitor said nothing. But his grip on Hailey's wrist tightened painfully and she realized he was scared.

For her own part Hailey was struck speechless. Her eyes and mouth gaped open and she stared and stared like a moron.

This room they'd entered was some kind of research laboratory. Only the research in here hadn't been conducted on animals, but on people. The laboratory was very large—about fifty feet by fifty feet square—and its left and right walls were bordered with ceiling-high cages in which the experimental subjects lay, stood, or crawled about on beds of bloody and filthy straw. The middle of the room was occupied by two large metal operating tables. A very weird-looking human corpse lay on the right operating table. The far end of the laboratory was occupied by a swimming pool, a six-foot-wide expanse of water separated from the room by a short tiled wall. Ripples and bubbles on the pool's surface indicated that this was the source of the splashing noises they'd heard.

Hailey vaguely absorbed this information about the room. She and her companions were however more preoccupied with the laboratory's hapless inhabitants.

All of the people in the cages had been mutilated in one way or another. Some had no arms, others had no legs. One man literally had nothing below his navel—his flesh was stitched up and two tubes projected from his back. Despite which he was horrifying, nauseatingly alive, his eyes gleaming brightly at them from the bottom of his cage.

Even stranger were the modifications that had been made to some of the captives. A good example was the weird looking body on the right operating table. The corpse looked weird because . . . well, it was actually *two* corpses stitched together, as if someone had been trying to create a set of Siamese twins instead of separating them. Here the 'twins' were a man and a woman. The mad surgeon had trimmed off the left half of the woman's body and the right half of the man's, then stitched the couple together. The madman clearly had a sense of humor, as he'd kept both sets of genitalia intact, the man's penis and testes on the left and the woman's vagina on the right, in essence creating a Siamese hermaphrodite. His mad creation lay there with one hand extended over each side of the table, both of its heads shaven and connected to wires that ran to strange machines which pulsed menacingly.

There were lots of machines in here, both near the walls and on mobile racks near the operating tables; and also some standing in the corners behind them.

Hailey and the others' entrance had caused a stir amongst the caged subjects, who were now all pushing against the metal bars and trying to reach them.

The captives weren't pleading for help however; and there were two reasons for this. Firstly, because all of their tongues had been cut out, and secondly because they were all gnashing their teeth *hungrily* at Hailey, Rhianna and the suitor, and reaching between the cage bars at them, their fingers clawing fiercely at the air. One man had arms which had somehow been extended to thrice-normal length and he was reaching out toward Hailey with them. Another 'man' opened his mouth and a thick tentacle like a toad's tongue uncoiled from it and flicked towards them. The tentacle had to be at least four feet long.

"Da fuck is this place?" Rhianna gasped in horror. "We down in hell or what?"

Hailey was trembling with fright. "I knew we shouldn't have come in here," she moaned. "I just knew it!"

And then the seemingly-dead 'Siamese' corpse on the right operating table twitched and they realized it wasn't dead. All three of them leapt back then and gaped at it. The hermaphrodite's chest began moving as if it was breathing, and its knees began flexing. The female half seemed to still be asleep, but even though his eyes also remained closed, her attached companion's lips curved up in a smile that Hailey found chilling. She was certain she saw evil in that smile, as if the twin's male half was listening to them and plotting against them.

"How the fuck do you sew two people together and keep them alive?" the suitor asked. "From what the doctors always say, there should be all sorts of medical complications."

"Beats me," Rhianna said.

Hailey turned away from the awful creature and instead found herself staring at a long cage filled with half-people. These experimental subjects were just head and limbs, their torsos surgically removed and their shoulders connected to their hip bones. How this was possible baffled Hailey. Who had done this to them?

The man in the cage next to the half-people had no facial features, that is until he opened his mouth, when Hailey saw that his nose, his ears and his eyes had all been moved inside his mouth, and that even though he had no tongue, he had ridiculously long teeth and his mouth was almost thrice the normal human size. His finger and toes had been replaced with long black claws that looked sharp enough to shred metal.

The deformed man saw Hailey staring at him and began dancing about like a chimp and scratching his crotch and his penis got hard.

Hailey bent over and threw up.

"Hey, girl, don't splatter me!" Rhianna yelped, leaping out of the way of the stream of vomit. But her words weren't really angry, she was too scared for that. It was impossible to be brave in here. All around them the products of a truly deranged mind beat and kicked against their cages, their obvious intent being to get out and attack and most likely eat these three intruders.

Hailey, Rhianna and the suitor clearly should have left by now, but there was a reason why, as horrified as they were, they all remained in the lab.

The thing was, that there *was* a ladder in the laboratory. It was over near the pool at the lab's far end, tucked away in a nook between the end of the left row of cages and a rack of machines, a nook that seemed to serve as a janitor's closet, because there were rags and a mop and broom shoved in there too. The problem was that the ladder was within reach of the man with the three-times-normal-length arms, who seemed to sense their need and seemed to be waiting for them to attempt to reach the ladder.

"Alright, girl," Rhianna told Hailey, "get over there and fetch that ladder and let's get outa here."

"You're crazy if you think I'm going over there," Hailey instantly objected. "Miriam Heller hired me to die for my virginity, not for my stupidity. You tired of living, you go fetch the ladder yourself."

"Listen, you head over there right now or I'll feed you to these damn things!"

"Forget it."

"Don't you dare me, bitch. I haven't forgotten how you killed that guy upstairs. You've still got an ass-kicking coming for screwing up my plans."

"Screw you, Rhianna. I'm not leaving this spot."

"Oh yes, you are!"

"Hey, let's not waste any more time in here than we need to," the suitor told Rhianna. "She's scared and I don't blame her. I'm scared too; none of what's been done to these people should be medically possible."

"But we need the ladder," Rhianna insisted.

He nodded. "Listen, I'll go get the ladder, it's just a short distance." Then he glanced ruefully down at his codpiece. "I just wish my damn dick would get scared too and deflate for a while. An erection ain't what I need at a time like this."

Widely skirting the table with the Siamese hermaphrodite, the suitor made his way across the laboratory. The man with the extra-long arms saw him coming and retreated back into his cage with a look of clear disappointment on his mutilated face.

"See? There was nothing to worry about," Rhianna told Hailey.

"So why didn't you go get it then?" Hailey retorted.

"Because I'm in charge here and I give the orders," the black girl retorted in turn, grabbing Hailey's right arm and squeezing it painfully.

The suitor had almost reached the nook with the ladder when something emerged from the pool at the far end of the lab and 'took' him. 'Took' was the right word, because the suitor didn't have a chance in hell of surviving it, not once the girls saw what had hold of him.

Alright, so maybe contesting on *The Virgin* show qualified as a surreal experience, and walking in here merely added to the nightmare quality of the bad decision Hailey had taken . . . but what came out of the water and attacked the suitor . . .

Well, for certain it had once been human . . . had apparently once been several humans in fact. It was long, with pale flabby skin that showed signs of having been stitched together just like the body on the operating table, though in this case, judging from the number of limbs the creature had (Hailey managed to count seven arms before it submerged again), more than two people had gone into its construction.

The four hands that grabbed the suitor were webbed like frog's feet and the mouth that instantly bit off the top of his head . . . well, the monster's head seemed to be three heads placed side by side and stitched together—it had three cranial domes, six neighboring eyes, and one long mouth that connected the whole mess from right to left. Maybe because it now lived underwater, it no longer had any noses.

The suitor gave one long shriek and then stood there jerking in the monster's grasp with the top of his head (everything above his nose) missing and blood dribbling down from there over his shoulders.

Then, with a mighty splash, the once-human thing vanished beneath the surface of the pool again, throwing a wave of water over the pool wall into the lab. It took the dead suitor with it, his feet first sticking out of the water and then slowly submerging.

Hailey began trembling. Rhianna, who was still holding on to her, let go of her and grabbed the nearer of the operating tables for support.

This was a mistake, because once the young negress was in range, the 'Siamese twin' creature lying on the operating table instantly sat up and grabbed her.

"Shit! Help!" Rhianna shrieked as the creature pulled her back towards itself, both of its faces now awake and grinning with hungry anticipation. Its mouths yawned open and Hailey saw what Rhianna (who was looking at her and not at the creature) could not—that this creature had long weird teeth like a movie vampire's.

"Help me!" Rhianna shrieked again as the hermaphrodite thing pulled her neck between its two heads and sank both sets of its fangs into her throat.

"Shit!" Rhianna gasped as the creature began draining her, streams of her blood dribbling down over her breasts as both of its heads sucked away. The wires previously attached to the twin's pair of shaved scalps had now detached from them and were dangling from their parent machines onto the floor.

Hailey certainly disliked Rhianna Jackson, but she wasn't about to sit aside and just let her die like this, so she hurried forward to save Rhianna from the creature draining her.

Realizing that she was endangering herself by doing so, she nevertheless grabbed hold of Rhianna's right arm and tried to yank her away from the 'Siamese twin.'

While doing so, her eyes scanned the room, looking for a weapon. Then she spotted a surgical trolley with some scalpels on it on the other side of the operating table.

All around them a huge racket was now ensuing as the caged captives, who'd been too cowed to demand a share of the thing in the water's kill, now banged on their cages, insisting on a share of Rhianna's flesh and blood instead.

Hailey stopped tugging on Rhianna's arm and started desperately for the scalpels. The 'twins' had a tight grip on Rhianna and weren't about letting go of their prey.

If I can just get one of those blades, I should be able to scare this creature into letting go of her.

She knew she didn't have much time to act either. Rhianna's eyes were already glazed and her mouth hung slackly open—Hailey just hoped the black girl wasn't already dead.

But then Rhianna kicked out, her flailing foot catching the surgical trolley that Hailey was reaching for with such force that the trolley slid over towards the cage containing the man whose face had been moved to the inside of his mouth.

The trolley hit the cage hard and Hailey didn't understand the mechanics of it, but the next moment, all the locks on the face-inside-mouth-man's cage sprung open and he was free of his confinement and coming at her with his mouth open and his claws extended to tear her up.

Hailey quickly backed away, tripped up and fell down. She thought she was done for, but the monster-man made a detour before reaching her. He stopped beside the operating table and ripped Rhianna's left arm off her shoulder, to the visible anger of the Siamese twins, who raised their heads from draining the black girl dry and hissed at him through tongueless mouths.

Rhianna, however, was already dead now. She must've been, because there was hardly any bleeding from where her arm had been wrenched off. The twins had sucked all the blood out of her.

The Siamese twins kept hissing at the face-inside-mouth-man and making threatening gestures at him, so he flung the severed arm at them and charged towards Hailey again.

Hailey though, was already back up on her feet and dashing out of the deranged laboratory.

She glanced back once and saw the deformed man coming out of the laboratory door after her, his mouth gaping open so he could see her.

A kind of panic that she'd never experienced before filled her as she fled from him. Her only hope as she ran was to reach the room they'd fallen into from the mall and lock its door. But the room was near the other end of the corridor and she doubted that she'd reach it before he caught her. And then what?

Another terrified glance back showed her two things: one, that the mutilated man was gaining on her, saliva now pouring from his mouth; and two, that he still had his erection, which he was gripping with one hand as he chased her down the corridor, not caring that his talons had cut through its delicate penile skin and were making him bleed on himself.

So he was going to both eat and rape her, though she wasn't sure in what order these atrocities would occur.

She got closer to the door she was heading for, and he got closer to her, while her legs strained to their limits, her heart pumped fiercely and her brain pondered the puzzle of how a few hundred feet could be so far away.

But just when she thought she couldn't run another step and was about to collapse to the floor, a woman stepped out of the room she was heading for.

It was Miriam Heller.

"Get down!" Miriam yelled at her.

Seeing the shotgun Miriam was pointing in her direction, Hailey instantly threw herself to the floor.

Next came a series of explosions and vibrations that seemed to reverberate forever along the corridor. Hailey flung her hands over her ears and shut her eyes.

Finally the noise subsided and she opened her eyes again. There were at lot more people in the corridor now: five or six Hi, Men! security guards, each of them armed to the teeth, and a man and a woman carrying video cameras.

She felt the gentle touch of a hand on her shoulder. "Hailey? Are you okay, Hailey?"

She nodded up at Miriam Heller. Miriam was no longer holding the shotgun, but behind her there was a mess of bloody meat on the corridor floor and wall which two of the guards were examining in confusion.

"Thanks for coming to get me!" Hailey gushed and clasped Miriam's prosthetic leg.

"You're welcome," Miriam replied. "We figured something was wrong when you three didn't emerge from that hole in the floor and the signals from your watches vanished. Looks like we got here just in time." She stared up and down the corridor, noticed the red octopus painted on its ceiling, and then pointed to the face-inside-mouth-man's remains. "What was that thing? And where are Rhianna and the man who was with you?"

Hailey pointed down the corridor. "Rhianna and the suitor are both dead. Please don't ask me how. And don't ask me what that creature was. You guys just walk down to that little open door at the end of the corridor and have a look for yourselves. There's something in there that you've gotta see." She realized she'd begun laughing. "Oh, you've gotta see this alright."

Miriam nodded. "Okay. Hailey, you wait right here, we'll be right back."

"Oh, I wouldn't leave this spot for half the money on the planet. And once you come back, just put me aboard the first chopper out of this place."

Miriam looked at her strangely. "It's that bad in there?"

"Oh, It's much worse. I'll gladly bet you a year's salary that you've never seen anything like what's waiting over there." Then she frowned. "Just one thing—don't any of you guys go near that pool at the far end."

Miriam nodded and stepped away from Hailey, who still felt too tired to get to her feet and who just sat back against the wall and stretched her legs out in front of her.

She watched Miriam organize the men and women with her. "Alright, Sapkowski, you heard what she said. Keep everyone on high alert and . . . Donna and Mark, make sure you catch everything on camera. And I mean *everything*."

"Gotcha, boss!"

They started off down the corridor, with Miriam clicking on a walkie-talkie: "Aaron, can you hear me? Darling, we've got a situation down here. We're likely gonna send up some footage covering Rhianna's death and that of one of the suitors, but don't put them on the show's live feed yet, not till we've had a chance to discuss it. . . . It's strange down here. The mall seems to have been built over some kind of underground facility. . . . No, baby, I haven't seen it yet, but we're heading there right now. . . ."

Hailey watched them all go. *As for me, I'm done with this crap. All I want now is that helicopter flight back home.*

Hailey's wristwatch vibrated for the second rest period. She ignored it. Instead she began laughing again, unable to believe that she'd just survived that nightmare.

CHAPTER 21

Miriam . . . The Final Rest Period . . .

The 'Siamese twin' creature was still sucking on Rhianna's neck when Miriam arrived in the laboratory. On noticing the new arrivals, it dropped the black girl's corpse and hissed at them, both its male and female heads baring long fangs surrounded by lips caked with blood. Neither mouth had a tongue.

Those images were instantly uploaded to the server and Aaron Heller's shock and confusion were obvious in his voice.

"Honey, I don't believe what I'm looking at down there."

Miriam looked around the laboratory, shuddered, and then replied into the walkie-talkie: "Trust me, baby, you're not alone."

"Damn, most of the crew monitoring the vid cameras look like they're gonna puke. Three guys have already run off to do so."

Miriam didn't comment. There was already a mess on the lab floor, from guards who similarly had been unable to keep down their dinners after walking in here. One man was still retching over in a corner.

She glanced around at the cages, at the mutilated and transformed people that they contained. Bar nothing, this was the craziest thing she'd ever seen. People surgically transformed into freaks? People with parts of sea creatures grafted onto them? Because, unless she was mistaken, that thing on that armless guy's back looked like an entire squid. And, from the way it was still moving its arms and tentacles, the squid was still alive?

Aaron's voice came over the walkie-talkie: "What I'm wondering is, who the hell did this?"

Miriam couldn't answer her husband's perplexed question. She wondered too. Staring at the cages' inhabitants was like being in a madman's zoo. It was as if the surgeon and creator of these monstrosities had disdained owning a normal menagerie and had decided to create one of his own, one inspired by insane nightmares in which he'd roamed through realms far beyond human comprehension.

Ever since she'd had her vagina surgically removed Miriam had wondered about the limits to the sort of alterations that could be made to the human body. *(If something that most women consider essential and vital to their well-being can be disposed of with minimal side effects, what else can we lose too?)* Judging from the experiments that had been performed here, there didn't seem to be any.

And yet . . . there was something more in evidence down here. This wasn't just butchery and insanity for its own sake. Miriam sensed a purpose to all this.

Take for instance, the Siamese Twin Vampire creature, which was thrashing about as three of the guards were strapping it down onto its operating table with arm and leg restraints obviously designed for that purpose, but either not employed or earlier loosened by the architect of all the human chaos here. To combine two separate humans into such a whole was beyond the limits of human medical science. The sutures combining the two bodies were almost healed and there was no evidence of either cell rejection or necrosis.

And the others—like the man with extended arms. In an adjoining cage sat two men without any arms and Miriam suspected that their removed arms had been used to lengthen the third man's. And the arms worked too—the man was hungrily reaching through the bars of his cage at a female security guard, with his fingers splayed to grab her. His blue eyes were bright with anticipation and he was licking his lips and drooling saliva down his chest.

Miriam noticed this and scowled. "For fuck's sake, Janice, stay away from that damn cage! How many times do I need to warn you lot to be careful down here?"

The woman quickly got out of the way. The man with extra-long arms looked disappointed for a moment, then he switched his hungry attention to another woman almost within range of his arms.

Oddly enough, this long-armed man had no penis. Miriam felt like gagging when she realized why: in another cage stood a man with a penis that had to be at least two feet long in its flaccid state. Looking around at several other castrated captives, Miriam easily figured out where the extra sexual tissue had come from.

They'd already had one casualty down here through carelessness. Their cameraman Mark had ignored the instructions not to go near the pool at the far end of the lab and the monster in there had gotten him. The thing that emerged from the pool had been a long and terrifying 'assembled' monstrosity with an excess of eyes and arms and a mouth like a shattered window filled with glass shards.

Mark's partner Donna had captured his gory death on camera. Mark's boots were sticking out of the pool, and his video camera lay on the ground beside it, but no one dared to go retrieve the camera.

The guards had been about to shoot the thing in the pool, but Miriam had ordered them not to. Mark was by then already dead anyway and she suspected that whoever owned this laboratory of horrors wouldn't be pleased if he returned and discovered his creations dead or destroyed. That once-human thing in the pool must have cost a lot of time and energy (not to mention finance) to create.

Oh yes, there was a lot of money involved in this. She gazed around at the lab's array of scientific machines, with their brightly flickering lights and glowing dials. Everything in here seemed state-of-the-art.

Yes, this crazy setup definitely cost someone a whole pile of cash.

Something that additionally horrified Miriam about all the malformed people in here was that they were all mad—without exception. The expressions in their eyes (that is, in the eyes of those that still had eyes) was merely one of intense lust for flesh to rend and eat and possibly also have sex with. They were all as insane as if the operations to transform them had been performed without anesthetic and their rational selves had fled their minds to escape the resulting unutterable agonies.

"Yes, Sapkowski, what is it?"

The head security guard had come over to her side. His black bike mask rendered him impassive, but his body language showed he was clearly rattled. "We found this in that desk over there," he informed Miriam.

She looked at what he was holding out to her. It was a thick file folder, but what interested her about it was the red octopus printed on the cover of the folder. Except her memory failed her, this was the same image painted on the corridor ceiling and—she glanced across at it but there was a guard in the way—on the lab door as well.

And this time there was a name attached to the image. "ROC (Red Octopus Corporation) Bioresearch Files.

Hmm, Miriam thought. *Now this gets even more interesting. It's not just one madman responsible for this then, but a whole group of madmen. Who are these guys? Neo-Nazi scientists or what? Aaron's dad was a Nazi hunter in his youth; he might find this interesting.*

But she wasn't allowed time to reflect on this new discovery. Her husband's urgent voice came over the walkie-talkie.

"Honey, the rest period's half over. What are we gonna do with all this stuff down there?"

Miriam checked her watch. "We'll seal the lab off until after the show. The show must go on, no matter what." She nodded at the head guard. "I'll take the file upstairs when I leave and examine it later."

The man turned away from her and she resumed her radio conversation with her husband: "Aaron, we've a small problem down here. But before we get into that, have you figured out what to do about Rhianna's death? She was the show's top-rated contestant and now this?"

"Relax, we'll run the footage as it is. Not the entire lab, just the bits you filmed of her in the monster's grasp. No need to explain how it happened. I'll have Tom splice it together with the previous footage of the three of them falling through the floor. No problem there. We'll back up a bit to where you're all out in the corridor and take it from there. Or maybe we'll show them everything from where you went underground. Either way, the viewers are certain to love it, they'll think it's all one of our booby-traps." He laughed. "The only person who's gonna hate it is Sheik Khomeini, who's fallen head-over-heels in love with Rhianna."

"Okay, that's fine," Miriam agreed. "What about the dead suitor? As far as I can tell, he's in the pool over there, along with Mark."

"Damn, we always did warn Mark to be more careful. Now look what's happened. Listen, honey, we'll leave the suitor out of it."

"People are going to wonder what happened to him."

"Well, we could . . ."

"Could what? Aaron, we've just six minutes left till showtime."

"I was thinking that we could CGI Mark's death as the suitor's death. What I mean is, we'll use the footage of Mark getting killed, but replace him with the other dead man. But . . . the problem with going that route is that lots of our viewers are tech-savvy, and if they detect that we faked that scene, the show gets a bad rep, 'cos then there's the question of how much else have we been faking. And you know that so far everything on our show has always been a hundred percent legit. What you get is what you see."

"Hmm, okay, I agree with you on that and—"

"And besides, once Hailey emerges from the hole alive, everyone's gonna forget about the suitor anyway."

Miriam felt a moment of tension when the freak with the elongated arms nearly snared another female guard—why the hell couldn't they simply keep away from him?—then she said: "Aaron, Hailey *is* the problem I earlier mentioned. The girl says she wants out." She sighed. "She wants to leave and I can't say I blame her. One of the damn freaks almost ate her too. I arrived just in time to blow his head off. Ugh, baby, you should have seen him. That one had his entire face packed inside his mouth—his eyes, his nose, his ears—the whole shebang."

"But, honey, she *can't* leave. If Hailey leaves it screws up the betting odds and folks will want their millions back."

"So what do we do? She's out there now waiting for a helicopter to take her home. We can't make her compete against her will. That isn't much different from murder."

"No, we won't force her. We motivate her."

"Darling, *how do* we motivate her?"

Aaron laughed. "We merely increase the prize money—appeal to her sense of greed."

"Can we afford it?"

"Oh, sure we can. Most of the smart money was on Rhianna Jackson to win again, and now that she's out of the running, we're making a killing this year. So we won't miss a few million dollars extra."

"Okay, I'll talk to Hailey. Two minutes to showtime. Love you, baby."

"Love you too, honey."

Miriam took a final look around the laboratory, then walked briskly towards the door.

"The file folder we discovered, ma'am," the head guard Sapkowski said.

She took the folder from him. "Secure the lab. Nothing gets in or out of here without my say-so."

"Yes ma'am."

She took a step through the doorway and paused again. "And Sapkowski . . . ?"

"Yes, ma'am?"

"If the guys who did this turn up during the show, don't you dare shoot them for any reason. You just give them my phone number and ask them to call me ASAP, okay?"

"Yes, Mrs. Heller."

That settled, Miriam left to go have a little heart-to-heart talk with Hailey Osborne.

CHAPTER 22

Hailey . . . Ten Minutes Later

Wow, how greedy am I?

Hailey still couldn't believe she'd let Miriam talk her into continuing on *The Virgin*.

But she made me an offer I couldn't refuse: The prize money is now fifteen million dollars, not ten! Fifteen million if I win. And like she pointed out, there's only one hour of game time left. Hailey checked her watch. *No, make that fifty-four minutes. In fifty-four minutes I'll be a rich woman.*

Miriam had driven Hailey over to the top of No. 5 Street. Streets Number 1, 2, and 3 were henceforth to be cordoned off and made inaccessible for the rest of the show.

"None of the other six remaining contestants are there at the moment," Miriam had explained as Hailey was getting out of her military-style Jeep. "Everyone has been notified of the changes by their wristwatch." Then she'd smiled at Hailey and melodramatically punched the air. "Good luck, girl. Fight for the money and for your hymen!"

Hailey had nodded and watched her drive off. Looking back across the point where the five game zone roads converged, she could see security guards at the entrances to the three blocked-off streets.

The summer night had turned cold and Hailey had wished she had something warmer than this bikini to wear. For a while, she watched a drone perched on a roof, watching her in return. Her upper lip ached where Rhianna had punched it open.

Then she'd looked down at the machete and knife she was holding on to and had remembered what 'fighting for her hymen' actually entailed. The familiar fear had returned and made her question her motivations for going on with this insanity of a game show.

Oh, I'm out of the fire and back into the frying pan!

She'd realized that standing out here in the open made her a fantastic target for Annette's arrows. She'd quickly ducked beneath the same oak tree she'd hidden behind earlier when her flight from Rhianna had brought her up here in the first place.

Then she'd begun making her way back down No. 5 Street.

***

There's just seven of us left now? Four guys, three girls?

Hailey's initial thoughts on realizing this were delighted ones. If there were so few people left, then how hard could it be to evade them and win, if not the whole prize, at least a part of it? She'd happily share with any other winners.

Dying isn't worth it. And besides there's a lot more money now, enough to go around.

But fate had other plans for her.

The first glitch in Hailey's plans came when she checked out the location of the nearest chapel on her watch. When she 'tapped for map,' the map revealed to her that now only one of the four chapels was in the newly shrunken game zone; the other three lay in the cordoned-off area (which was represented by a red grid drawn over everywhere west of No. 4 Street).

"Oh, dammit!" Hailey growled in frustration.

The sole chapel now available was at the other end of the game zone, down at the bottom of No. 4 Street.

Well, beggars couldn't be choosers. Hailey had already worked out a plan of action for the next—she checked her watch—forty-eight minutes:

I'll just hang around there by the chapel; skulk about in the shadows. I won't enter any of the houses so I don't trigger a booby-trap and I also won't drift too far away from the chapel. I won't use it immediately, but if anyone starts chasing me, I'll know where safety is.

She'd hoped for at least two chapels, so she could shuttle between them; but with that option gone she'd make do with what she had.

Hey, when other people are looking for you and you're trying to avoid them, does that increase the likelihood of you encountering them or does it reduce that possibility? Hailey hoped it was the latter.

She made her way past a suspended monitor which was replaying Rhianna's death. She winced as she watched the 'Siamese twin' holding Rhianna close with its fangs sunk deeply into her neck, though by then Rhianna was clearly dead, her head hanging slackly forward with a thread of bloody spittle dangling from her spread lips.

Then, in a scene taken with an overhead camera she saw several skeletons down in the laboratory pool. All had been stripped clean of meat. And then the thing in the water came up and the onscreen images exploded into white light.

Hailey hurried past the monitor as Rhianna's death replayed. She quickly figured out what she'd just watched. Someone had hit on the idea of using a drone to record the thing in the laboratory pool, and the creature hadn't liked being watched. End of drone.

***

Hailey was about a third of the way down the road when she began hearing noises. Somewhere a woman was singing loudly.

Who the . . . ?

Hailey did the only logical thing: she detoured from her trip to have a look.

This required her walking in between two houses and tracing the source of the sound. It was not a recording, that was for sure.

She finally found the singer. It was Annette Morrison.

Annette was sitting in one of the fake-houses. The front door was wide open and so Hailey just stepped through it and saw her.

This fake-house seemed to be a tailor's shop, or maybe it was used for upholstery. In addition to the ubiquitous boxes of 'stuff' that Hailey had come to associate with such buildings, there were several sewing machines and also large bolts of fabric and imitation leather placed against the walls.

Annette was sitting at one of the larger sewing machines. A few yards away from her lay two completely skinned corpses. Hailey immediately understood that the bodies belonged to dead suitors because both of them had arrows in their heads. One corpse had an arrow through its forehead and the other had an arrow through its open mouth.

Piled on the floor like fabric beside Annette were the dead men's skins.

Annette was sewing their skins while singing. The song was Slain Jane's *Ballad of Erin De Mornay*—which Hailey knew used lyrics from

The Bleeding Oysters, a novel by the 'vanished' writer Drake Melville, whom Slain Jane's lead singer Janet Orgasm had briefly dated:

> "Her pain begins this wedding night,
> Eternal misery with no end in sight,
> A marriage of torment and fetters,
> The silly girl ought to know better!"

Annette was singing this chorus with gusto as she fed the skin through the sewing machine and Hailey admitted that she had a lovely voice. But what she was doing?

"Ugh" Hailey bent over and vomited. She just couldn't hold the puke in.

The noise alerted Annette to her presence. Annette turned and smiled at Hailey. "Oh, Hailey, darling, I'm so glad you could drop in."

Hailey managed to straighten up and wipe her mouth dry with the back of her hand. She already regretted stopping here and was prepared to bolt for safety, but Annette showed no sign of reaching down for the bow and arrows on the floor beside her. Instead, Annette seemed genuinely pleased to see her.

"What the hell are you doing?" Hailey enquired, while trying not to vomit again. Even after all she'd witnessed in that nightmare underground lab, the sight of the two skinned men in here was a lot to take; even their faces were gone. "Why are you . . . ?" She gestured helplessly at what Annette was up to.

"Oh, I'm just making my wedding dress," Annette brightly explained. "It's lovely, isn't it? Just a few more stitches and I'll be done."

Hailey was stumped by the reply. "A w-we-wed-wedding dress?"

Annette nodded. "Surely you remember the song lyrics:

> She wore a wedding robe of human skin,
> Then her husband and his infernal kin,
> Dragged her down to their realm of sin,
> And she was never seen again . . ."

She looked expectantly at Hailey, who nodded warily back. It was the second verse of that same song *Ballad of Erin De Mornay.* Hailey had read Drake Melville's novel; all of her friends had. They'd also all come to exactly the same conclusion about Mr. Melville: that the man was completely insane and better off missing and never found.

Annette resumed stitching contentedly.

"So what's the dress for?" Hailey asked, because that was the only question that came to her mind. She was very conscious now of the fact that Annette was batshit crazy.

Damn, I realized that the first time I saw her, but this . . . If she makes the slightest move for that bow of hers, I'm out of here like a flash. Though armed, she entertained no delusions of taking Annette on woman-to-woman. *Crazy people are known to be extraordinarily strong!*

"Oh, I just feel like a demonic bride tonight," Annette proclaimed joyously. She stepped on the sewing machine's pedal and the sheet of skin flowed beneath the needle and dropped towards the floor on the machine's other side.

"But what about the competition?" Hailey asked.

"Oh, I love this competition!" Annette replied. "I'm having so much fun tonight!"

"Okay, I'll be going then." Hailey nodded and prepared to leave.

"Wait!" Annette said, her eyes gleaming bright as lamps. "I'm just about to try my wedding dress on." She stood up and stretched. "Tell me how you like it and help me zip it up."

Hailey waited. *Yes, curiosity did leave the cat with just eight lives, but I have to see this.* And also, being in here with Annette was helping run down the show clock—just thirty-nine minutes left now—and if Annette had been in here for a long time there might not be any booby-traps in here, meaning this house might be a safe place to hide in till the show's end.

I don't mind sharing the prize money with Annette, she thought while watching the older woman strip off her bikini, revealing in its full glory a body surprisingly perfect for her age, *so long as she's taken straight from here to a lunatic asylum. In fact, I'm going to insist on her being committed.*

Now naked, Annette hauled the mass of sewn skin towards her, parted a hole in its middle and stepped into it. She began pulling her gory, stitched creation up her body.

Hailey didn't want to see this, so she looked away, and when she did so was when she caught sight of the telltale white cord running up one of the room's rough pillars. That could only mean one thing: booby-trap! Her eyes nervously followed the cord up through the missing ceiling and amongst the rafters. Finally she located the hidden cage. There were actually two cages up there, and from the muffled motions inside them, Hailey was certain that there were more of those poisonous giant spiders packed inside them.

That changed her opinion of this room. *No way am I hiding in here! They must like Annette 'cos she's—*

Annette's voice cut through her thoughts and she looked down again.

"It's a little bit tight around the bust. But I don't have time to adjust it again."

Hailey just nodded and stared. Annette had actually reduced her to speechlessness. She stared down at the two skinned bodies on the floor and then back up at Annette again.

She actually did it—she's sewn a wedding dress from their skins!

The 'dress' was a gory tapestry of insanity and had no logic to its construction. Well, that was the impression one got when looking at it, mainly because there was no other way to view a piece of 'clothing' where one man's nipple was stitched next to his navel and both of these were set over the wearer's left hip, while the other navel was positioned over the woman's right knee and there were two more male nipples down by her left toes. One expanse of male buttock skin covered Annette's chest and cradled her breasts (with its anus looking like a pendant hanging between them), the other was positioned over her own buttocks and dangled tassels of blonde scalp. The rest of the 'wedding dress' was just as crazily constructed. Both men's penises and testicles were stitched on at its shoulders like military epaulets.

But for all that, it *was* an actual dress, with sleeves formed from one man's legs and a long bloody bridal train made from both of their arms and hairy armpits and a brown-haired scalp.

"It's a bit messed up," Annette apologized, "but I was in a hurry." She smiled nicely at Hailey. "Zip me up?"

Feeling that if she'd come this far, she might as well go the whole way, Hailey nodded. She walked behind Annette and took hold of the zip. Then, in a fresh wave of dismay and nausea, she saw that the dead men's faces had been stitched on either side of the zip, and she leapt back again.

"Sorry, I can't!" she yelped, and before Annette could enquire what the matter was, she'd run out of the house.

"What a silly young filly," Annette pouted after her, then she giggled in delight. "Oh well, I'll just have to manage this myself then. And oh, where did I put those lovely earrings I made?"

*****

Hailey wasn't really thinking when she emerged on the street again. She figured she had just over half an hour left to survive. As far as she could tell, Annette had mentally quit the competition over that 'wedding dress' nonsense of hers.

Which left just Teresa—late Rhianna's 'trailer trash princess'—to deal with. Hailey wondered where Teresa was now.

I don't care where the hell she is. I'm heading down to the chapel and that's that. In twenty minutes it'll be safe for me to enter the chapel and wait there till this is over.

But right then she saw three suitors coming up the road towards her.

Oh shoot! There was no way forward now. The only thing to do was to dash back between the houses, which once more took her past the house where Annette was now admiring herself in a mirror and lustily singing:

"Once I was a princess virgin,
With a pussy full of yearning.
And now Prince Charming is coming,
Yes, he's coming inside me,
His cock so hard and sperming!"

Hailey winced at the Slain Jane lyric and kept running.

CHAPTER 23

Teresa

Teresa was in a lot of trouble and the damn handcuffs were responsible.

The suitor she'd been stalking (because he had a set of handcuffs and she wanted his keys) had turned into this house and she'd followed him inside.

Once inside they'd gotten into a fight, which Teresa had lost . . . and now she was lying duct-taped on a table and about to be deflowered.

The irony of this was that the suitor had removed her handcuffs before securing her wrists because the cuffs interfered with his placement of the duct tape.

Teresa considered her current situation to be a completely unfair twist of fate. *Hey, I just watched Rhianna's death! That should have made me the favorite to win this.* Well there was Annette to consider; but Teresa hadn't seen the librarian for at least an hour. *So maybe she got caught and eliminated from the show and I missed it. Hey, I need this damn money to change my life?*

She was lying on her right side on the tabletop. The suitor had taped her wrists together and also her ankles. Then to limit her range of motion and also to prevent her from being able to free her hands with her teeth, he'd bound her wrists to an additional loop of tape below her knees.

Teresa was trying her best to free her hands. But it seemed impossible; she couldn't twist her fingers into a position where she could grip the end of the tape and peel it back.

This looked like the end of the road for her hymen.

The position she was in, lying on her side, and bent forward with her legs pressed together, meant her captor would have no access to her vagina from the front, but she was completely open to him at the rear.

She lay there, fearfully anticipating the horrible moment when he would walk behind her and enter her young body.

This house had loads of cartons in it and the suitor was rooting through them, looking for something. He was a short man, the same height as Teresa, but was much more muscular. As he bent over an opened carton, she admitted that he had a great ass, but that wasn't the important thing now.

"I just wish those damn rats would stop making that racket," the suitor said. "The sound of 'em is almost driving me nuts!"

This was the first that Teresa had heard of the rats. Now she listened and wondered how in the world she hadn't noticed their noise too. She decided it was because she was used to rats: for her, hearing them squeaking and pattering about everywhere was like using a white noise machine to help you sleep. Thrice when she was in high school and her drunk of a father had gotten sacked (yet again!) her mother had set traps inside their trailer and the rats (real big rodent bastards too) had smelt the bait and come in through the holes in the trailer floor and had all wound up in the oven—lots of meat for the family until her father had sobered up and found himself another job.

Of course, eating rats because you were dirt-poor wasn't the kind of thing you told your friends about, it was like eating dog food because you were broke. But it was much better than eating roadkill raccoon like her sister Martha was once forced to do when she was seven month's pregnant and her own drunk of a husband (both of Teresa's elder sisters having seemingly made a point of duplicating their mother's marital mistakes down to the last gene) had run off to Bridgeport in West Virginia (supposedly in search of a job, but actually to see his ex-girlfriend, whom he'd wound up getting pregnant too).

Now that she was an adult, Teresa Coombs was amazed that her entire family hadn't died of the plague back then. Eating rats? Had that been reckless behavior or what?

Anyway, the point is that Teresa wasn't scared of rats. And now that she'd heard them, she could suddenly smell them too—a thick, if faint smell.

The suitor, however, was having a fit. The man had now found what he was looking for, a yellow tub of something that he held in his right hand, with his body posture indicating that he'd love to throw it at the rats, if he could just locate them.

"Shit! I wish those things would shut up!"

Teresa now began wondering where the rats were. They sounded like they were below her, but that seemed impossible: the floor was made of seamlessly joined laminated wooden tiles.

She quit thinking about the rats. She had major worries of her own. The suitor had just placed the yellow tub by her right shoulder. She saw that it was a tub of I Can't Believe It's Not Butter spread. And next, he opened it up and began lubricating his right hand with the spread, coating his fingers and palm with it as thickly as if he was buttering a slice of toast.

"What are you doing?" she asked in horror.

He laughed, his voice deep with bass. "I'm about to deflower you, sweetheart."

She gaped at him. "With your hand?" She nodded toward his codpiece, at the stiff and fat penis inside it which, positioned on her side like she was, was now staring her right in the face. "Why not use your dick?"

The suitor stopped buttering his hand and sighed. "Because this penis is a fake, sweetheart." Teresa was about to protest, but the man placed a buttered finger across her lips to silence her and then, while she spat the margarine across the room, he quickly undid his codpiece's clasps. He dropped the wire-mesh codpiece to the floor and then pulled off his penis.

Teresa gaped some more. This man had a vagina between his legs. A very hairy vagina with fat lips and a massive clitoris. It was right before her eyes and undeniable.

With a shriek of horror she went limp on the table. "I'm about to be fisted by a transsexual," she groaned aloud. "It figures."

"You got a problem with me?" the man asked angrily. Now, with that bird-head on him and that hairy vagina, he looked like one of the harpies of legend. She noticed the pair of faint horizontal scars below the man's pectoral muscles, clearly souvenirs of having his breast tissue removed.

Teresa couldn't help but reply sarcastically. "No, no, please go ahead and fist me. But has it at least occurred to you that if you try fitting your entire hand into the body of a young woman who's never been penetrated before, you just might kill her?"

"Nonsense. I've fisted lots of women and they've all had orgasms."

"Man, how many of them were virgins?"

"Aw, shut up. You're not getting out of this whatever you say."

Teresa was going to suggest that he PLEASE use his artificial penis on her, but the man had already resumed coating his hand with I Can't Believe It's Not Butter.

But then the suitor growled, "Why won't those damned rats shut the fuck up?"

His angry comment set Teresa thinking again. *Where are they?* Possibly because she was so distraught, the rodents now sounded like they were everywhere around her—like they were trapped inside the room's walls. The creatures sounded very agitated, but their sound was also a distant one. It was perplexing: the rats' smell was right there with both of them in the room, but it also appeared to be coming from a distance.

A booby-trap? Teresa wondered. *Is there a rat booby-trap around here? But if there is, where's its trigger?*

"Alright, let's get this hand into you, sweetheart!" the suitor said with glee, his voice taking on that really deep pitch again. Teresa would never had guessed that he'd once been a woman—the guy looked more masculine than many guys she knew. She figured he was in the competition to earn the money for his Sexual Reassignment Surgery.

But he's not earning it from me!

She got a final look at that hairy, masculinized vagina and then he'd turned away from her and was walking around the table.

Next stop, my backside. Bound up as she was, Teresa saw just one route of escape from her current straits, even if it would be just a temporary one. She hooked a hand on the edge of the table, and then, with a massive tug and twist of her body, rolled herself forward and off the tabletop.

She'd made her move just in time, as she'd felt the suitor's greased fingers touch her buttocks at the instant she'd rolled.

"What . . . ?" came the man's surprised gasp from behind her as she crashed to the floor.

The impact half-stunned Teresa. She lay there getting her wits back. The next move of her plan was to roll backwards and get under the table. But before she could do this, she realized that she'd finally worked out where the rats were.

They were underground. With her ears pressed to the floor she could hear them down there under the wooden tiles, scampering about, shrieking in frustration and rage, flinging their hairy bodies about. They sounded hungry . . . very hungry.

The suitor had now stepped around the table and was staring down at her.

"What the hell is wrong with you, girl?"

He reached down for her and she bit him. She bit his hand hard, so that his blood filled her mouth. And then when he jerked his hand away and went to get his knife, she quickly rolled under the table like she'd planned.

"I'm gonna really fuck you up now!" the suitor grunted angrily.

Teresa stared at him. He'd retrieved his knife, but was examining the blood welling from his fingers.

"Dumb bitch!" he said. Then he growled "Look at me!" at her, and wiped off his bleeding fingers against his sex, so it seemed like he was bleeding from his vagina. "When I'm done with you, sweetheart, you're gonna be looking exactly like this!"

The image of having her own sex reddened like that, with blood on her thighs, terrified Teresa. Having her period was one thing, but not like this.

Shit, where's the trigger to the booby-trap!?

He took a step towards her, knife raised.

Then she saw it—a white cord emerged from the floor and looped around a small pulley set into the side of the table leg by her head. The cord rose halfway up the table leg and ended secured to a nail. Clearly the way to trigger the booby-trap was to shift the table, which yanked the cord. She also worked out that, here beneath the table, she was out of the trap's range: she could still hear the agitated rats, but they were no longer directly beneath her.

The suitor had just bent down and taken hold of Teresa's feet. "Alright, come on out of there, you!"

Instead, she squirmed forward, stretched her neck the rest of the way and took hold of the cord with her teeth. Then she jerked on it as hard as she could.

"What . . . !?"

She heard a click in the floor beneath her and let go of the cord. She was facing outward and so saw a section of the wooden floor split open and fall inwards.

Vanishing like a magic trick, the suitor went down into the pit.

Teresa lay there relieved, but she couldn't relax long, because a few moments later, the screaming started. The man's anguished voice started off as deeply masculine, but within seconds it had transformed into something genderless akin to the cries of a mortally wounded animal.

Teresa dragged herself to the edge of the pit and peered in. Then she vomited over its edge.

The pit was about eight feet deep and its bottom was packed with huge rats—these ones were even larger than the ones Teresa's mother used to catch for dinner.

The rats were eating the suitor.

The man was trying to fight them off and get to his feet, but the giant rodents must have been starving for days, because they swamped him. When he managed to get to his knees, Teresa saw that the rats had already tunneled into his belly. One black rat ripped off bloody shreds of the man's labia, then dipped its head deep into his vagina to feed, while another was stripping his right forearm clean of flesh. The man's bird-mask had been half eaten away; its long beak hung down over his bloody chest. His left eye was a bloody hole. A rat had affixed itself to his left cheek, its teeth sunken deep into the bleeding meat. She watched another leap up onto his right shoulder and sever his ear with a single ravenous bite.

The weight of starving rats pulled the screaming suitor down out of sight.

Teresa vomited again on the mass of rats and then she rolled away from the pit.

The dying man had dropped his knife outside the pit while falling into it. Teresa wearily crawled over to the knife and began cutting herself free of the duct tape.

CHAPTER 24

Annette

If asked why she was still a virgin at her age, Annette Morrison would say (just like Hailey Osborne would) that it was because she'd just not yet met the right man.

But the truth was even stranger. 43-year-old Annette was one of those women who are blessed (or cursed) with a very rugged maidenhead. After five attempts with various lovers to rupture her hymen had failed, rather than have it done by her doctor or simply puncture the offending tissue herself with her fingers or a vibrator, Annette had decided that her vagina was destined for something extra-special and had given up on losing her virginity altogether.

The fact that she had some really weird ideas—with all the books surrounding her in the libraries she'd worked in it was only a matter of time before she became deeply enamored of mysticism—only helped reinforce Annette's conviction that her virginity was something to be treasured and reserved for an intense and worthwhile event.

For something just like this contest.

And reading Drake Melville's 'marvelous' *The Bleeding Oysters*? Oh, that had been a once-in-a-lifetime epiphany; an irreproducible moment in time when she'd understood her own true nature.

When Annette finally experienced her big defloration, she wanted an immense stage, with a band playing and bells ringing. Figuratively speaking of course.

But she also wanted that ten million dollars in prize money, wanted it even more in fact than she wanted the other. So it didn't look like she'd be losing her 'innocence' tonight, which she felt was very sad, because most of the masked suitors were very hunky.

"Aw well, a woman can't have everything," she consoled herself.

***

Annette sat on her waterbed and played with herself. She knew there were cameras recording her every motion and this she desired.

The waterbed was a big one and she lounged in it like a queen. This house was built like a chalet, this bedroom as luxurious as a hotel suite, with fridge and bar and lots of cushions.

She was still wearing her wedding dress of human skin, to which she'd now added both thick slutty makeup and earrings made from the eyes of the two men whose skins she was wearing; one blue and one brown eyeball dangled from each of her ears.

Her wristwatch told her there were just thirty-three minutes left.

"Time to get this show on the road."

Knowing this would be her performance of a lifetime, Annette began singing loudly, in that sweet contralto voice that had attracted Hailey to come and investigate it. She'd left the bedroom windows open and knew that her voice carried out far into the night. As she sang she masturbated, thrilling her flesh but not allowing her physical joy to spill over into orgasm.

Her bow and arrows lay on the plaited quilt beside her and occasionally she stroked them like she stroked herself.

Annette waited.

Soon she heard voices: "She's in here!"

She stopped playing with herself and picked up her bow. She fitted an arrow to the bow, pulled back on the string, and waited some more.

Then, like a bird arriving at a birdbath, a suitor walked into the bedroom. Annette still couldn't get over how ludicrous these men all looked. Whose idea was this anyway? Demon masks would have suited the suitors better.

Still, this man was black and tall and under any other circumstances, she'd have happily granted him a chance at breaking open her pubic restriction zone.

"Hello, darling, goodbye, darling!" she greeted him cheerily and then let the arrow fly at him. But the man flung himself to the floor just in time and the deadly shaft flew over his back and streaked out into the hallway.

She smiled. *No problem, darling; I've lots more. I'm still gonna make a porcupine out of you.*

Annette calmly reached down for another arrow, but before she could pick it up, she was seized from behind by two sets of hands.

"Alright, hold on to her! And get those arrows away from her."

The men must have entered through the window to the en-suite bathroom or through a rear door that Annette hadn't noticed. She struggled a little, but then gave in gracefully, like a queen would.

"Alright, you can have them," she said and let go of the bow. The weapons were quickly taken away from her and dropped out in the hallway.

Only now did her three captors (the third man having gotten up from the floor) pay close attention to her clothing.

"Dude, she's crazy!" the black man said. "She's wearing Jimmy's skin!"

Annette smiled and stroked the Lone Star Flag tattooed on the patch of skin over her right hip. "Oh, was that his name?"

"Oh man, you're right!" another suitor said. "How the hell can anyone do shit like this? She's actually sewed their skins into a dress."

"Yes, this is my lovely wedding dress."

"Man, I feel like I wanna puke."

With her weapons gone, they'd decided she was harmless and stood or sat staring at her. They made no attempt to restrain her—now *they* had axes and machetes and she had nothing. She clearly wasn't going to be able to escape all three of them.

But yet, they stared at her in awe. Annette knew they were terrified of her because of her wedding dress. And because of her lovely eye-earrings. She looked exactly like the demon's bride in *The Bleeding Oysters*. Made up like she was, she looked like the devil's favorite slut and she loved it.

But the show must go on, she thought. *And now that it's clear that I won't be winning that ten million dollars tonight, I'm going to have me some carnal fun.*

So she laughed. Her outburst of mirth was so sudden that all three of her captors leapt back from her and looked about to flee if she made the slightest of motions towards them.

She did consider attacking them, but then she changed her mind. Her sex felt red hot from the masturbating she'd been doing in here and the moment suddenly felt right.

"Yes, great deeds are at hand!" she intoned grandly at the men like one reciting a script at an audition. "If my hymen's time has come, then alas, so be it. But the wedding dress stays in the picture? You'll have to kill me to take it off. Deal?"

The three men nodded slowly, though none of them took a step towards her. They were still too frightened of her; they thought she was about pulling some trick on them.

So Annette lay back on the waterbed with splayed legs, pulled her skin-dress up over her hips, and pulled her labia brazenly apart with her fingers so they could see the pink ring of virgin flesh they were here to destroy.

Then she sang at them: "Come and get it, boys! Dinner's ready, come and get it, boys!"

Few men could refuse an invitation like that, even though the woman was wearing two other men's skin. These three men finally began removing their codpieces.

Maybe Annette's hymen had grown weaker as she'd grown older, but this time it gave way on the fourth or fifth thrust, and after that she seemingly couldn't stop coming.

CHAPTER 25

Miriam

Miriam scowled at the images her composite control room monitor was feeding her. She'd expected more from Annette, not this damn orgy.

Lady, you're supposed to fight tooth and nail to keep your cherry, not give it away like a Christmas present.

But, watching the ballet of writhing bodies, she couldn't deny that Annette's performance made great TV. Their underground show's online rating had jumped up several notches once the gangbang had commenced, and when, after all three suitors had had her once, Annette had lustily groaned, "Boys, I want all of you in me at the same time—one in my pussy, one in my mouth and one in my ass!" the ratings had blown through the roof.

This year's *Virgin* show had now officially broken the underground internet.

(Just like the scene when Rhianna had been bargaining with the suitors, this one also had sound. There were hundreds of microphones in the game zone, but the logistics of their placement meant that except in rare cases one only got noise or static.)

Miriam grudgingly conceded that for a newbie Annette Morrison was vastly gifted where group sex was concerned, and she planned on suggesting a career in porn to her once the show ended. For sure, the MILF community would eat her up.

Her stump itched and she absentmindedly scratched the point on her left thigh where flesh and blood ended and plastic and steel began.

What about us? she wondered. *We've cleaned up this year and don't really have to go on with this . . .*

But of course there would be another show next year. The underground fans would demand it, and the thought of all the money to be made would make she and Aaron seek out yet another set of desperate young women with a piece of priceless tissue to sell.

But . . .

She glanced right. She'd been trying to put off looking through the file folder with the red octopus on it until after the show, but now she was forced to consider the implications of what they'd discovered in that underground lab where Rhianna Jackson had met her death.

I can't shake off the feeling that this organization intentionally left those freaks down there so we'd discover them. But why would they want us to discover them?

It was a question as yet unanswerable. Later she and her husband would sit down and reason through all this and then thoroughly investigate this ROC organization.

"But right now I've a show to finish," she said aloud, forcing her attention back to the huge composite monitor that dominated the front wall of her Control Center.

The inset countdown clock said 2:33:16. Twenty-seven minutes left. Miriam smiled wistfully and hoped for a violent blood-and-guts conclusion to the show like they'd had last year. Last year's *Virgin* show had actually ended early, with half an hour to spare, but everyone had been very impressed by its shocking finale.

I really hope we get something just as good this year. Too bad Rhianna died when she did. Are Hailey and Teresa up to providing a fitting climax to this year's show? I don't think so, but we'll see. Twenty-five minutes. Hmm, this is the time when contestants' desperation makes them do crazy things.

She focused. Onscreen, Annette was still hard at it. Now she was riding one suitor reverse-cowgirl while masturbating the other two. She looked grotesque in that skin-dress of hers, but there was no denying that it gave the whole orgy scene a wonderfully macabre touch, not least whenever the man behind Annette grabbed the faces that made up the back of her dress to steady her on his erection.

Two side monitors showed Teresa and Hailey. Both young women weren't doing much, just walking in the same direction down adjacent streets with several buildings separating them. Hailey, naturally the more timid of the two, was a few yards behind the other girl in her progress, but neither of them was aware of the other's presence forty yards away.

Miriam was mightily impressed with how Teresa had worked her way out of her last dilemma. Now there was a young virgin worthy of emulation.

Unlikely granny here, who's banging three suitors like she's making up for lost time. Or Hailey, who seems headed in that southern direction simply because there's a chapel down there where she can hide.

At the moment Teresa had the dead transsexual suitor's fake penis stuck in her makeshift belt. *Hahaha! I wonder what the dirty little virgin plans on doing with that big dildo?*

A niggling worry took Miriam's attention away from watching Hailey and Teresa and focused it back on the sex show Annette was putting on.

There was something about this room she was looking at that disturbed her.

The black member of the trio of suitors was ejaculating on Annette's face. The squirted drops of come missed her eyes, hit the center of her forehead and from there dripped down alongside her nose to her mouth and the tongue which greedily lapped them up.

I'm certain that room is booby-trapped, but where's the trigger? This is a very delicate situation here—three suitors inside—and I need these guys to take on the last two girls . . .

She scratched her leg stump again and tried to concentrate. There were eight luxurious bedrooms in the game zone. Four of them had traps and four of them didn't. Was this one of the clean ones or wasn't it? She had to know.

"Hey, Aaron," she said into the air, her senses suddenly tingling in alarm from some obvious but forgotten danger.

"Yeah, honey, something the matter?"

"Aaron, this is important. This room where Annette's having her porno shoot—"

Aaron laughed. "Yeah, real great, right? Everyone utterly loves it—the response is through the roof. In fact, Sheik Ibrahim Khomeini is already asking if she's for sale . . . apparently he's never married a librarian before either."

Miriam rolled her eyes at the old Arab's persistence in acquiring exotic wives, particularly American ones. "Tell him she might be, if they can agree terms. But that's for later. Right now we've a problem." She went on quickly before he could interrupt her with a follow-up witticism: "Darling, is this room one of the *clean* ones?"

Aaron didn't know either. They had a department that set the booby-traps. "I'll check," he said, suddenly catching some of her nervousness.

She waited with baited breath for him to confirm her fears.

On-screen, the sex had finally stopped. Annette and two suitors lay on the waterbed, while the third man had just emerged from the bathroom and was walking towards the small fridge. All the men's erections had deflated somewhat, but not totally. The man making his way to the fridge was almost fully hard again.

"Anyone thirsty like me?" he called out to the others.

"Yeah, dude, I'll have a Coke," the black suitor said.

"Monster Energy for me," the other suitor said. "And then we need to go find the last two girls. We gotta pop those cherries before time runs out."

"You're leaving me then?" Annette asked sadly.

"Just for a half hour, baby," the suitor near the fridge said. "But if we don't go out and earn some money now, we ain't gonna have the cash to show you a good time later."

"Oh, alright," Annette agreed with a lazy smile. Miriam had the sudden impression that all of the older woman's 'crazy' had been the result of not having fucked a man for over twenty years. That could be expected to drive any normal hetero woman nuts.

"You want a drink too, baby?" the man by the fridge asked Annette after pulling out a Coke from a middle shelf and placing it on top of the fridge beside the can of Monster Energy and his own Coors Light.

Miriam wondered what was taking Aaron so long to get back to her. She had the feeling she was watching a disaster unfold, only it was building up in slow motion, tantalizing her with its inevitability and daring her to stop it if she could.

This is crazy, she thought. *I'd better send in security to get them all safely out of there.*

"Yes," Annette replied the suitor, "I'll have a beer. Get me one like yours."

"One ice-cold beer coming up," the man said and reached down into the fridge again.

Aaron's voice came over the intercom then: "I've checked. The room *is* booby-trapped. The trigger is in the fridge. A beer on the top shelf connects—"

He never finished the sentence because two things happened simultaneously as the suitor pulled Annette's beer out of the fridge.

First of all a circular wall of glass shot up out of the bedroom floor and completely encircled the waterbed; and next, the waterbed itself exploded.

And that was it for Annette Morrison and the black and white suitors trapped in there with her.

Because as Miriam suddenly remembered, that particular waterbed wasn't actually filled with water, but with highly concentrated acid, and the bed itself had been constructed from one of the two flexible plastics that the acid couldn't corrode.

Annette and two suitors began screaming as the acid splashed over them, and their screams only got louder as the acid melted away their skin and flesh, quickly revealing the bones below and then eroding away those bones too.

Annette did try to escape, climbing on the head of one of the suitors (the man's skin was so corroded by now that Miriam couldn't tell if he was the black or the white one). The skin suit had provided Annette with an additional layer of protection, but still, her face had melted like it was candle wax, and her once-lovely lips were dripping off her teeth like bloody spittle. Her black hair had dissolved into bubbling red irrigation ditches all over her peeled scalp, and her arms looked like overcooked sausages that had split from the pressure of their contents. Most of the flesh on her feet was already gone when she stepped up on the suitor's head and reached for the top of the glass enclosure, which remained tantalizingly out of reach, mere inches from her desperate fingertips. But then her foot bones punctured through the top of the dead man's corroded skull and, screaming in agony and terror, she slipped back down into the dissolving mess of flesh and soon became one with it too.

The suitor standing by the fridge was visibly trembling with fright. Then he turned and bolted from the room. In his fright, the man ran off without either codpiece or weapon.

Miriam vomited. When she trusted herself to speak again, she said, "Aaron, find the psycho sonofabitch who suggested this booby-trap and fire him before I kill him."

Her husband's equally shocked voice came back over the speakers. "Actually, honey, it was your idea."

"M-m-my i-i-idea? "She stared in horror at the melted human remains in the glass circle. What remained of Annette and the two men looked like cake mix. "I-I-I s-s-suggested th-th-this? No, I-I-I know I didn't."

"We were both drunk that night and trying to think up the most horrible ways to kill people . . ."

Miriam nodded. "R-r-right. Well, it sure as hell looks like we succeeded."

She was relieved when the monitors switched focus.

With both young women completely forgotten in the insanity that had just claimed three lives, Teresa Coombs had just captured Hailey Osborne and was dragging her into a building near the No. 2 Street Chapel. A side monitor showed the suitor who'd survived Annette's meltdown walking dazedly in the two girls' general direction.

Miriam checked the time. Eighteen minutes left.

"Now *this* looks like an interesting conclusion to the show," she told her husband as the software tracking the two virgins switched to cameras inside the house.

She focused on Hailey and Teresa and did her best to forget how horribly Annette Morrison and the men had died.

I was responsible for THAT? Oh, my dear God, please forgive me!

CHAPTER 26

Teresa

Teresa dragged the struggling young woman after her.

"Shut up and quiet down or I'm gonna cut you!" she growled, pressing her knife into the side of the other girl's neck and drawing some blood.

Hailey quieted down then, her angry protests becoming subdued whimpers.

Teresa was very pleased with the fright in Hailey's eyes. Her fear would make things easier. She was scared too after watching the screening of Annette's death, but not so scared that she hadn't noticed Hailey staring at another monitor like a rabbit transfixed by headlights.

Grabbing Hailey and disarming her had been simple; the girl only seemed to realize her plight when Teresa pulled her past a white shed with a blue cross on its front door.

"Oh, the chapel!" she'd gasped with longing, stretching her hands out towards it, and then she'd begun kicking and scratching and trying to get over there. But Teresa wasn't about letting go of her. She'd placed her knife against Hailey's pale throat and dragged her along.

Well that was over now. Once they were both inside the building, Teresa kicked the door shut and looked around.

This house they'd entered was a carpentry shed: lots of wood stacked against the walls, two sturdy worktables and lots of saws and smoothing planes and other tools hung on pegs on the wall. There were shelves of nails and bolts and screws and hinges and handles and also boxes of electrical fittings. There was sawdust all over the floor. Two half-finished chairs stood in a corner beside a pile of blue foam. Several coils of rope dangled from hooks.

Remembering how she'd escaped from her last captor, Teresa

looked around for any cords that might be hooked up to booby-traps. Finding none, she relaxed a little.

After quickly making up her mind on what she was going to do with her captive, Teresa roughly shoved Hailey toward one of the worktables. This one was mostly bare; the other had several tools on it, including a nail gun and a circular saw.

"Hey, let me go!"

"Behave yourself or else!"

"Listen, just listen to me," Hailey protested. "You don't have to do anything to me. There's enough damn money to share!"

Teresa snorted at the suggestion. "Share? Share fifteen million dollars with you when I don't have to? Are you nuts!"

Hailey looked at her as if *she* was nuts to not want to share that much money, and this angered Teresa, brought a lot of repressed rage to the surface of her mind.

"Just shut your damn trap," she growled at Hailey, pressing the knife to her throat again, "or I'll make sure I hurt you."

She pulled the dildo from her belt and waved it in Hailey's face. She loved the look of dread that came into the other girl's eyes when she saw the plastic penis. Her scared gaze seemed to ask: "Is this sex toy gonna rob me of seven-and-a-half million bucks?"

And the answer to that thought, biatch, is yes, Teresa thought coldly. She was aware of time passing—just fifteen minutes left by her watch— and there was still that one remaining suitor out there to deal with. It would be utter misery for her if after disposing of Hailey's hymen she got caught and deflowered too.

But now that Hailey's pointed out where the chapel is, once I deal with her, I'll hide in there till the clock runs down.

"Now bend over the table and spread your legs, biatch. I'll try to make this quick and painless."

She shoved Hailey face-down over the table and then spat on the dildo. She didn't really want to hurt the girl; she just wanted the damn money. *Imagine her suggesting that I split it fifty-fifty with her. Split that much loot? She's nuts!*

She spat on the dildo again. "Alright, now relax and it shouldn't hurt too badly."

Instead Hailey spun around and elbowed her in the face. Teresa felt a jolt of pain rock her head. Then blood squirted from her nose and she knew that the little bitch had broken her nose. Staggering back, she flung the dildo away. Hailey was staring at her as if she didn't believe what she'd just done.

"Why you!" Teresa spat at her. "I'm gonna—!"

She lunged at Hailey and grabbed her around the throat and began throttling her. Hailey tried to grab her throat also, but she had shorter arms and couldn't manage it. So instead she took to punching Teresa in the breasts, which hurt like hell, but Teresa refused to let go. Moving back and forth as they struggled, they soon reached the second worktable, the one with all the tools on it.

Teresa didn't know that Hailey had found a weapon until pain exploded in her left arm.

She looked down in horror. Hailey had stabbed her in the bicep with a screwdriver. Now she was bleeding from her arm as well as her face.

She let go of Hailey's neck. Gasping for breath, Hailey staggered back. "Look, you can have all the damn money!" the girl said. "I'm not about dying over this!"

But Teresa was too far gone now to listen. She was utterly enraged. Now she understood why Rhianna had sliced that other girl's head off last year: some uppity bitches just *had* to be put in their place. She saw clearly how one could reach a point where one threw all considerations of right and wrong out of the window.

Hailey must have seen the murderous look in her eyes, because she turned to run. But Teresa wasn't about letting the little scheming bitch leave. Because once she got out of here, she was clearly heading for the chapel down the road. And once there, with only thirteen minutes to go, she'd be safe, invulnerable. Teresa would have to share the prize money with her, and she wasn't ready to do that.

Hailey was already opening the door when Teresa grabbed her by her hair, rabbit-punched her so she was stunned and then pulled her back toward the worktable. Blood was streaming down Teresa's face and arm but she ignored the bleeding.

Oh, biatch, I'm about to make you bleed too.

Once she had Hailey's back pressed against the worktable that had the tools, she grabbed up the circular saw and powered it on.

Hailey stared at her dully as she brought the whirling blade near her face. "So you wanna be a millionaire too, biatch? I'm gonna show you exactly what happens to girls who try to take my money."

Hailey's eyes widened with fright again. She seemed great at getting scared.

Teresa smirked at her and waved the circular saw. "Yeah, biatch, I'm gonna deflower you with this. Only, unlike the nice little dildo, this saw is gonna cut through most of your crotch as well!"

Pushing Hailey back over the worktable, Teresa swung the saw down to begin cutting. She was just about touching the circular saw to Hailey's flesh when she felt a nasty blow to her head and staggered back again.

Half-stunned, she looked up in confusion. Hailey was holding the nail gun (which must have been what she'd hit her with) and was trying to work out how to power it on.

Teresa raised the saw and charged at her.

But she was too disoriented to attack effectively and merely got clobbered in the head again with the nail gun. The circular saw went flying from her grasp and she collapsed over the table unconscious.

***

When Teresa awoke a short while later, she found herself locked in place, seemingly unable to move.

Confused and still groggy from being hit twice in the head, she at first tried looking down her body, trying to understand why she couldn't move her feet, but she was bent too far forward over the worktable to see beyond her hips.

However, both of her feet felt stuck in place. As did her hands.

Hey, why can't I move my hands? she wondered, lifting her head and looking at them. Her arms were pulled well forward (so she was forced flat on her belly on the table) and her hands were turned palm-down on the wooden tabletop and also locked in place. But she saw no sign of either a rope or duct tape or handcuffs keeping them where they were.

Huh? What's going on here?

She shook her head to clear it fully, and then finally noticed Hailey, who now stood on the opposite side of the worktable and was waving a large white tube at her. Hailey's fingers covered most of the writing on the tube, but Teresa did make out the damning words 'INDUSTRIAL STRENGTH CYANOACRYLATE ADHESIVE.'

And then Teresa understood why she was now immobilized: *This little mousy biatch has SUPERGLUED my hands to the worktable and my feet*

166

to the floor! I'm gonna kill her for this!

Shocked, Teresa tried tearing her hands free, but they were stuck rigidly in place; she discovered that Hailey had also superglued her wrists and her forearms to the tabletop. All Teresa got for her efforts to free herself was horrible burning pain as if her flesh was about to peel off of her bones. She quit trying; combined with the pain from her broken nose and stabbed arm, her agonies seemed too much to deal with simultaneously.

She realized also now that Hailey had positioned her perfectly for rear-entry sex, had bent her over the worktable with her buttocks free and her legs spread wide. Arranged like this she was opened up for whoever wanted her. The little biatch had even taken off Teresa's bikini. Looking down her body again, she was horrified to discover that Hailey seemed to have also superglued her bare breasts to the table.

She noticed that Hailey was staring at her and frowning coldly. "Looks like the money's all mine now, bitch," the girl said.

"Please," Teresa pleaded. "Don't do this to me."

The other girl smirked at her. "Don't you dare ask me for pity. I was going to split it evenly with you, but not after what you were about to do to me. You were gonna slice me in two to win?" She shook her head in disgust, pointed to the nail gun, and added, "You should be grateful to me: for a moment I thought of nailing your hands and feet down . . . but I really don't hate you that much. So just take what's coming to you—I win, you lose."

Teresa began weeping. She didn't know if she was weeping from the fear of losing her virginity or because she was losing the prize money so late in the game. Or maybe her tears came from the sheer embarrassment and indignity of being stuck here like a rat on a glue board or the insect 'tenants' of a roach motel.

CHAPTER 27

Hailey

Hailey opened the door and peeked outside. Just as she'd hoped, alerted by the noise they'd made during their fight, the last surviving suitor was coming down the side street. Then she looked past him to the monitor at the junction—which now showed Teresa's broken and bleeding nose—and realized that he must've have watched their fight too.

Weirdly though, the man wasn't wearing a codpiece and his only weapon was a short two-by-four.

She waved to him. "Hey, over here! We're running out of time!"

He looked at her cautiously, then started over, his bird mask and bared erection making him look absurd.

But she was in no mood to laugh. When he reached her, she stepped back inside the house. She was pointing the nail gun at him and knew he wouldn't dare attack her.

"She's all yours," she told the suitor as he stepped past her. "Me, I'm going to wait here by the door and watch. I'm not about losing seven-and-a-half million dollars 'cos you didn't get the job done right." She pointed to the dildo on the floor. "If *you* don't break her open, I'm going to use that."

"No need for that," the man said, his penis throbbing with readiness. "I'll get it done."

Hailey checked her watch and then gestured over at Teresa who was now weeping copiously. "Hurry up, man, we've only eight minutes left. If I'm right, in addition to winning all the suitors' money now, you're going to get a two hundred grand bonus for her cherry."

"Damn right!" Dropping the two-by-four, the man hurried over to Teresa and got behind her. He spat on his erection and lined it up with her slit.

"Hey, don't you dare put that nasty thing in me!" Teresa moaned when she felt the penis at her entrance, though to Hailey's ears her plaintive cry seemed to have a mixture of resignation and repressed lust mingled in it. "I'm warning you, man. Don't you dare fuck with me!"

"Do it, man!" Hailey growled at him. (She'd noticed that Teresa had said 'don't fuck with me' and not 'don't fuck me.' *Now is that a Freudian slip or what?*)

"SHIIIIIITTT!" Teresa howled when the suitor rammed his member home with a single thrust. She trembled on her glued-down feet and tried to tear her glued arms loose from the worktable.

The suitor began thrusting. Teresa began making "OH, OH, OH!" noises.

"Ouch, that stings! Ouch, ouch . . . OUCH! Hey, slow down, you sonofabitch!"

"Hey, don't you dare slow down!" Hailey growled in response. "And don't go easy on the bitch either. I want her more open after this than the Mass Pike."

Feeling strangely aroused by Teresa's ongoing defloration, Hailey walked close to them. She wanted to make sure of this.

There was very little blood, just a few red specks on Teresa's buttocks. This made Hailey peek more closely to ensure that the man was actually in Teresa's vagina and wasn't mistakenly tearing up her anus.

And then, seeing that the deed was being properly done and knowing that she was a rich young woman now, she backed away from the copulating couple.

Teresa was resigned to her fate now; she'd stopped weeping and just looked pissed off. "Hey, hurry up and come already!" she growled at the man. "You don't have to spend all night at it!"

"No rush, baby," the suitor calmly retorted. "I'm really enjoying this tight hole you got here. And your ass ain't bad to look at either."

Hailey was amused. *Time to go.*

Along the way, she picked up the suitor's short two-by-four from the floor, and when she got outside the house, she nailgunned it across the front door, ensuring there was no way the man could change his mind and come after her before she made it to the chapel.

Four minutes more.

Hailey walked to the chapel, let herself in, and sat down before the blue cross to wait out the last few minutes of *The Virgin*.

She felt pleased that she'd won.

She felt even more relieved that she'd survived.

CHAPTER 28

Hailey . . . One Week Later

"Hi, Bern!" Hailey called brightly.

Bernie Murphy, the guy who lived in the apartment above Hailey's, paused on the landing and waved back at her. "Hi, girl, how're things with you?"

Hailey, who was just coming in from the supermarket and was poised with her key at the front door of her apartment, grinned at him. Bern was cute, very cute, tall and dark and handsome. Unfortunately he was also dating Amanda, a girl who worked at the Walmart Supercenter with Hailey.

No, Hailey quickly corrected herself. *I USED to work at the Supercenter with Amanda. I no longer work there; I quit on Monday. At the moment I'm a young millionairess!*

Bern was still smiling at her. But there was sadness in his smile. "Hey, don't tell me," Hailey said, "Amanda's left you again."

He nodded. "I don't know what it is with her. We seemed so happy this time, and then this morning she just started packing her stuff into her bags and . . ."

Hailey nodded sympathetically. "She'll come back again, Bern. I know she will." Amanda broke up with Bern at least once a month. She'd be away for about a week and then come running back saying she couldn't live without him.

"Wanna go out for a beer later?" Hailey asked Bern. "It'll cheer you up."

He nodded. "Yeah, sure. Better than staring at the walls and wondering what the hell I did wrong this time."

"Okay. Come by at eight then."

On that note they parted. Bern shuffled off up the stairs and Hailey let herself into her apartment.

***

Hailey Osborne had quickly discovered the two drawbacks to having lots of money: firstly, you suddenly discovered that you now needed lots of stuff you hadn't needed before becoming wealthy; and secondly, you couldn't work out which of those now necessary things to buy first.

The email message informing her that she'd won fifteen million dollars in the online Maidens Lottery had come in the day after she'd won *The Virgin* game show.

A few minutes later, her bank had sent her an email confirming the deposit of the money into her account.

And for the six days since then, Hailey had been buying stuff.

Not expensive stuff, just things most young women her age considered essential: clothes, clothes and more clothes, shoes and handbags and yet more shoes and handbags; jewelry, perfumes and lots of makeup.

At the moment her house looked like a boutique and shoe store, which she found amusing since she wanted to own a boutique and shoe store anyway.

She'd also ordered a few sex toys online. Most lay about in boxes, but she had tried out one new model vibrator and it was just . . . wow! Like someone was giving her head.

She hadn't yet decided on which model of BMW to buy.

Hailey currently owned six iPhones of different colors and was wondering in what daily order to switch her solitary SIM card between them.

This last run to the shops, however, had been primarily to purchase groceries.

I'm gonna need a bigger place, she thought with a wide grin while threading a careful path through scattered clothes to her kitchen.

She dropped the shopping bags on the kitchen counter, got out a soda and popped the tab. She took a deep gulp, looked back out through the kitchen door into her living room and giggled. Having money was fun.

Also, all this buying Hailey was doing was helping her forget the hell she'd gone through to earn her money. Even now, she still winced a little whenever she sat down. Teresa's circular saw *had* nicked her labia; but the cut was mostly healed now.

And there were lots of other things she'd seen on *The Virgin* that she'd like to repress into the dark vaults of memory: things like watching a two-headed Siamese vampire draining the blood from someone; things like watching three screaming people dissolve into mush in an acid bath; stuff like a roomful of surgically redesigned people, including one man whose entire face had been moved inside his mouth.

Sometimes at night this face-inside-mouth man chased Hailey through her nightmares, his penis hard and dripping blood. Once she'd woken up screaming.

So each day Hailey shopped to forget. And the cure was working.

Shopping *is* therapeutic. Ask any woman.

Hailey hadn't yet told anyone about her winnings. She didn't intend doing so until she'd worked out what she was going to do with it all. She'd seen enough TV shows about lottery winners to know that the moment people found out about her new wealth, she was going to be besieged with all sort of requests for money, even from folks she'd never met before.

I'll just take my time and I'll be okay. And hey—Mom and dad have wanted to travel the world for years, but never could because they didn't have enough money. Well, guess what? Now THEY DO have enough money! Hahaha!

Yes, she was fast realizing that a whole lot of things that had once been way out of her reach were now within easy grasp of her fingertips. Being wealthy unlocked all sorts of doors for you.

And of course, one thing leads to another. Now that Hailey was wealthy, she wanted a young man to share the wealth with.

A nice young man like Bern upstairs, for instance. Someone with a good job who was stable and who knew how to take care of a girl. She knew Bern was smitten with her and would be all over her if only Amanda wasn't in the picture.

Of course when she found her own young man, Hailey didn't intend telling him she was rich. She wanted him to love her for herself and then—

And then her phone beeped an email notification.

She pulled out the pink iPhone (oh, it was just so cute!) and tapped the screen on. She was perplexed to see that she had a new email message from Hi, Men!:

Hello Hailey,

We trust you are well.

We at Hi, Men! would like to again thank you for appearing on The Virgin game show. Once more we congratulate you on winning.

Now we have a request for you: We were so impressed by your performance this year, that we'd like to extend the offer to you to compete again next year. This of course will necessitate your remaining 'intacta' for the next twelve months, but we here at Hi, Men! are willing to compensate you with a million dollars up front for any inconvenience such celibacy may cause you . . .

Hailey finished reading the email. Then she set down her phone on the kitchen countertop, and seeming to forget all about it, wandered back to the living room with her can of Sprite in hand.

They want me back again? Seriously? Hahaha! Yaay!

She sat there considering the pros and cons of such a move. *I've already got fifteen mil, if I accept this offer that makes it sixteen, and I stand to win another ten next year—that's twenty-six mil. Oh my God, that's wonderful! I'm gonna do it!*

But then one of the images she'd been 'shopping to forget' flashed before her eyes—the dusky Rhianna Jackson's terrified face when that 'Siamese twin' monstrosity had clamped both sets of its fangs into her throat and started draining her . . .

Suddenly, all of Hailey's enthusiasm for a repeat appearance on *The Virgin* deserted her.

A strange panic settled over her.

Suddenly it became not a question of *if* she wanted to lose her virginity, but *how fast* she could be free of it.

She got up and strode back into the kitchen. She closed the email from Hi, Men! She'd reply them later. But for now . . .

Bern replied on the third ring. He sounded a bit sleepy, which was cool. She wanted him in bed anyway. The good thing here was that, with Amanda gone again this morning, Bern wouldn't be cheating on his girlfriend. And Hailey only needed him for a short while anyway. She'd be out of Bern's life by the time Amanda wanted back into it.

"Hi, Bern," she said. "Hope I didn't wake you up. . . . No, I'm not cancelling our drinking date. . . . Dude, I've got this little problem that I need you to handle for me. . . . No, I can't tell you what it is over the phone, but can I come upstairs right now? I'll explain in detail once I see you. . . . No, it's not an emergency . . . well, yes it is an emergency, but not a 911 kind of emergency. . . . Okay, I'll be right up. . . . Hey, and Bern, you got any wipes at home? . . . Oh, it's just that I might bleed a bit."

That settled, Hailey hurried into the bathroom to touch up her makeup. Then she left her apartment and hurried upstairs to lose her virginity.

CHAPTER 29

Miriam . . . Two Hours Later

Hi, Men!

Thanks but no thanks! Sorry to disappoint you, but I couldn't wait any longer!

Yours cheerfully and CHERRYLESSLY!
Hailey

Miriam Heller scowled at the reply Hailey Osborne had sent her: The girl had even had the nerve to upload a snap of her penetrated passageway—the reddened vagina wide open and completely unblocked, not to mention dripping with semen to boot.

Miriam felt so traumatized by the sight of Hailey's destroyed hymen that she left her living room for her bedroom, where she sat for a few minutes staring meditatively at her own bottled and preserved womb and vagina.

Doing so usually calmed her and it worked this time too, though at first the stump of her left leg seemed to throb in sympathetic anger. Still, after a while she felt the power of her pure virginity flood and soothe her.

After staring at her bottled private parts for five minutes, Miriam felt strong enough to return to her living room.

"A letter for you and your husband, Mrs. Heller. It was delivered by courier five minutes ago."

"I've told you to call me Miriam," she replied Teresa.

"Sorry, Miriam, but I keep forgetting," Teresa Coombs replied politely. At the moment she wore a transparent half-mask to protect her broken nose while it healed (she looked like the Phantom of The

Opera's younger sister), but the doctors had assured her that she'd be back to normal in no time.

Teresa was now Miriam Heller's P.A. The position had been open for a while and Miriam had offered her the job once the show ended, and while the understandably distraught girl was still superglued down over the workbench in the carpentry shed and the workmen were trying to unstick her, a job which had taken them two full hours to accomplish because they'd had no acetone on hand.

Miriam really liked Teresa—the girl reminded her of herself— someone willing to fight for what she wanted.

Not like that Hailey—she forced thoughts of Hailey's now-gaping sexual opening from her mind.

Too bad that Teresa hadn't won. But the consolation prize was alright too. The young woman was no longer trailer trash, her new six-figure salary more than saw to that. And at the moment, save for that gothic plastic mask on her face, she looked like an actual princess, with her perfectly styled hair, her exquisite manicure and pedicure and her long blue dress. The dress's long sleeves hid Teresa's healing chemical burns from the superglue.

(Jessica Fox, the third surviving female contestant, was still in hospital. The spider venom had fucked up her brain. Unfortunately, 'daddy's little girl' was going to be something of an idiot for the rest of her days.)

Miriam took the letter from Teresa and waved her to a chair. "Have a seat while I read through this. And afterwards I'll drive you to the clinic for today's scheduled checkup on your nose."

"Thanks, Mrs. . . . I mean, Miriam."

But Miriam didn't hear her reply. She was staring at her letter. While it was unusual enough to receive a personal letter in these days of instant email, it was even more unusual to receive one embossed with the image of a red octopus.

But there was no mistake. Their names 'Aaron & Miriam Heller' were printed on the envelope.

Miriam's lips were dry as she opened the envelope. For the first three days after the show, she and Aaron had done a lot of research concerning the ROC or Red Octopus Corporation, i.e. the persons who owned that insane basement laboratory. In the meantime they'd had to look after all the freaks down there—they couldn't very well let them starve to death. And most of the freaks only ate raw meat.

Well, it had been a good way of disposing of the dead suitors and of Rhianna's remains too.

Two days ago Aaron had sent the ROC an email asking them what they wanted done with their grotesque creations.

And this apparently was the reply. Only it was also something much more than a mere reply.

With bated breath Miriam unfolded the letter and read:

Dear Mr. and Mrs. Heller,

We of the Red Octopus Corporation are delighted with your interest in our organization.

As you suspected, we did indeed leave those experimental freaks down in the mall basement in the hope of your discovering them and that you'd afterwards contact us.

Our reason for doing so? It just happens that for a while now we have been considering producing a show along similar lines to your recently concluded 'The Virgin,' which we must admit we found most enjoyable this year.

We intend to call our own show 'The Final Girl' and wonder if you'd be interested in both organizing and hosting it for us . . .

Miriam Heller smiled and mumbled a quiet, "Yes, of course we will," to herself. Then, waving the letter at Teresa, she burst out laughing.

Teresa Coombs looked startled at first, but then, deciding the boss is always right, she laughed along with Miriam.

The End.

ABOUT THE AUTHOR

Wol-vriey is Nigerian, and quite tall.

He believes there actually are things that go bump in the night.

He writes horror fiction—for adults only, please. And also some surrealist stuff.

Wol-vriey blogs at: _http://oddityfarm.wordpress.com_

WOL-VRIEY
BIZARRO AND TRANSGRESSIVE FICTION

BOSTON POSH (BUD MALONE #1)

In 2028 AD, the USA is a nation ravaged by hungry dragons and dinosaurs. In Boston, Massachusetts, private eye Bud Malone is hired to rescue a kidnapped heiress. But nothing is as it seems.

Malone works to unravel a tangled web involving Boston Chinatown, a 200-year-old woman with a 9-year-old body, white robots, a human-liver-eating psychopath, a golem, a porcelain dragon, and a snake goddess with a crush on him. There's also a woman obsessed with chicken sex. Then Malone meets Posh Lane, a gorgeous call girl who's desperate to quit her pimp.

Romantic sparks ignite between Posh and Malone, but Posh's past suddenly catches up with her in a BIG way. To save Posh, Malone agrees to run a quest for Earth's new rulers, the Forks. But, Malone has no idea that agreeing to the Fork's odd request will send him on the weirdest trip he's ever been on in his life.

BOSTON CORPSE (BUD MALONE #2)

MAGIC CAN BE MURDER! - Drag queen Lucy Tang is back in Boston, and is hell-bent on settling her vindetta against casino owner Sookie Ling. And suddenly, Bud Malone, PI, has the case of his life to resolve.

When Boston's robot police force are baffled by a mind transfer case, they come to Malone for help. The one person who can likely help Malone out here is the witch Soledad Bathory. But Soledad seems to know a lot more than she's telling him. It's a case not made easier when Malone meets Soledad's beautiful cousin, Josephine 'Slave' Bailey. Slave has her own plans for Malone, most of which involve teaching him BDSM and making him her new Master.

Oh, and Rick Rogers owes Sookie Ling a whole lot of money, a gambling debt that's going to be literally Hell to pay!

BOSTON CORPSE - Not your average detective novel!

Burning Bulb
PUBLISHING

WOL-VRIEY
BIZARRO AND TRANSGRESSIVE FICTION

BOSTON LUST (BUD MALONE #3)

"Bless it, Father, for she has sinned."

Seven murdered gay women, all their bodies completely drained of blood. All also with large parts of their bodies dissolved away like acid has been pumped into their veins.

Bud Malone has to find the female vampire preying on Boston's lesbian population.

Then Malone meets the beautiful Trudi Carmen and the case gets even more tangled. Trudi needs Malone's help in recovering a ring that's gone missing. But how in the world is one little black ring related to either the dead women or their killer?

Resolving this case will lead Malone deep into Lucy Tang's legacy—The Abstracta. And then to the city of Genesis.

Boston Lust—Just when you thought Bean Town was safe to visit again.

HELL DANCER

Six people find themselves trapped in Detention, a nightmare realm where the demonic Schoolmaster is hell-bent on reforming them . . . until they die.

Porn superstar Venus Deluxe came to Springfield, MA to party, and next found her life hanging by a thread. One wrong answer will mean her death.

Suspended BPD detective Tanya Rockford was trying to stop one kind of violence, but found a terrifying another. With her and her companion's lives hanging in the balance, it's going to take all of her courage and resourcefulness to escape this hell she's stumbled into.

Porn stud Chad Cannon has made a career from his ten-inch penis. Here in Detention, however, it's his brains that matter. He'll soon be hoping all the pot he's smoked over the years hasn't completely messed up his memory.

The three students, Sherri, Jordan, and Mike? They were all just in the wrong place at the right time. Will anyone survive Detention? The evil Schoolmaster doesn't plan on letting that happen . . .

Burning Bulb
PUBLISHING

WOL-VRIEY
BIZARRO AND TRANSGRESSIVE FICTION

VAGINA MUNDI

Rachel Risk is a professional thief with super-strong hair that can stretch like tentacles to manipulate objects. Ashley Status has both a digitally augmented brain, and 'muscle-purses' in her arms and legs in which she stores inflatable objects—cars, guns, rocket launchers, etc.

When Raye is framed as the fall girl in a jewel robbery, the pair flee Chicago's vengeful robot gangsters and take refuge in the Hotel Bizarre, where the gorgeous 'vagina singer,' Femina, is performing for a week.

But the Hotel Bizarre is even stranger than its name suggests, and very soon Raye and Ash are involved in an deadly adventure, a struggle for survival the likes of which they'd never imagined possible—with loads of deviant sex, drugs, music, and violence at every turn. And just what is the old woman in the skin desert really doing with all those cats glued to her walls?

VAGINA MUNDI—a Bizarro Hymn in praise of WOMAN!

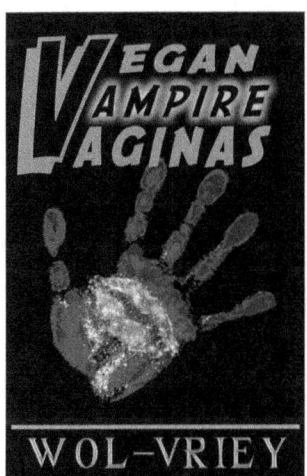

VEGAN VAMPIRE VAGINAS

The biggest bank heist in US history. And Tom Palmer can't remember pulling it off. And no, this isn't your standard case of amnesia. After a one-night-stand gone horribly wrong, Boston salesman Tom Palmer wakes up with a vagina implanted in his left hand. Then his day gets worse.

Tom is transported across space-time to a nightmare version of Boston, one where the Bizarro virus has transformed half the population into cannibals. Worst of all, Tom discovers that in this new Boston, he's the infamous gangster Pussypalm, wanted for robbing the Federal Reserve Bank of Boston a year ago. He also learns that the vagina in his hand is prophetic, i.e. it talks . . . after sex.

With 130 people left dead during his bank heist and six billion dollars missing, Tom knows he's living on borrowed time. It is in his best interests not to remember anything. Because once he does . . .

Burning Bulb
PUBLISHING

WOL-VRIEY

BIZARRO AND TRANSGRESSIVE FICTION

VEGAN ZOMBIE APOCALYPSE

In the post-apocalypse worlderness, zombies rule the earth. They're allergic to meat, and brains literally make them explode. Zombies now eat blood potatoes, parasitic tubers grown in the flesh of humancows corralled in maximum security farms. Two fugitives meet in the ancient ruins of Texas. The first is Soil 15-f, a womancow who's escaped her farm a week before she's due to be killed and her blood potato crop harvested. The second fugitive is Able Kane, former head necros food technician, now sentenced to death for heresy. But Soil is no ordinary humancow.

Unknown to herself, she's the vegan zombie agricultural revolution, and the zombies desperately want her back. And the necros equally desperately want Able Kane dead. He's fled with a forbidden discovery which will reshape the world for the worse if used. And Able is just hardheaded/misguided enough to use it.

MELANIE NEMESIS CATCHPOLE

In Springfield, Massachusetts, Melanie Catchpole is hired to fetch back a magic teddy bear worth millions of dollars from a warehouse across town. Problem is, the warehouse is down in Springfield's O-Zone—that totally weird sector of the city where Bizarro fell to Earth. The 'O' is a fairytale land, a place where dreams and nightmares literally live and breathe..

Worse still, the gingers—mutant cannibals—prowl the O. The gingers have already eaten everyone else Melanie's employers sent to get back the magic teddy bear.

Accompanied by the handsome but ruthless Doug Fisher (who she finds sexy but doesn't dare entrust her heart to), Melanie enters the O-Zone. Melanie and Doug are instantly caught up in an adventure they'd never have believed credible even if written as fiction . . . and Melanie's used to experiencing the very weird as the norm.

And now, additionally, there's a mystery to unravel: What does the dark, freezing-cold being called The Fixer want with Mary, the barkeep's daughter?

Burning Bulb
PUBLISHING

WOL-VRIEY
BIZARRO AND TRANSGRESSIVE FICTION

BIG TROUBLE IN LITTLE ASS

From Bizarro master storyteller Wol-vriey comes a truly weird western tale that will leave you awe-struck and on the edge of your seat...

In the town named Little Ass, tight-assed prostitute Rosa overhears a gunslinger's plans to assassinate rancher Edison Bennett. Once the badass Bennett learns of the plot, he ensures there'll be hell to pay for any attempt on his life!

Yes, it's going to take all of gunslinger Jude's shooting prowess, his eclectic collection of strange firearms, a trusty horse that requires an owners' manual, and the help of the lovely and invigorating Nell (who's EXTREMELY odd when the going gets weird), to survive the Bizarro hell that Edison Bennett unleashes in order to hold onto the land that he'd stolen from Madam Zizi.

BIZARRO 101 (A BASIC PRIMER)

Welcome to the strange place:

A collection of 37 flash fiction stories designed to introduce one to the Bizarro/New Weird Genre.

Weird, dreamy, nightmarish, absurd, sad, surreal, humorous . . . this collection of tales is all this and more.

***

"This primer is the very essence of any and all styles and types of Bizarro writing. Wol-vriey collects, distills, and bottles up these 37 tiny stories for your sensory enjoyment. This is an absolute must-read for anyone new to the genre, because it demonstrates the scope of what Bizarro is, and what it can be."
— Teresa Pollack, Bizarro commentator and blogger

Burning Bulb
PUBLISHING

WOL-VRIEY
BIZARRO AND TRANSGRESSIVE FICTION

Dr. Orgasm

Courtney Taylor is young, intelligent, beautiful, and successful. She also has a boyfriend who loves her deeply. The problem is, no matter what Courtney does, she can't climax during sex.

When Florence Rigid's communist forces destroy the city of Metaphor, Courtney and her friends Teresa, Highball, Miki, and Heather are cast into the midst of a quest to find the only person able to save the land of Innuendo—Dr. Carol Orgasm, wanted by the communists for developing the O-Pill, a wonder drug that grants women sexual ecstasy on demand.

The communists will do anything to get their hands on the O-Pill and prevent its reaching the millions of Innuendo's women. But Courtney desperately wants that pill too. And so it's now a race between Courtney and the communists to find Dr. Orgasm first.

And Courtney has no choice but to win this race. She must win it: For her own orgasm . . . and for the freedom of female sexuality everywhere.

PUSSY TRANSMISSION

Pussy Transmission were the most decadent Pop Art ensemble of the 90's. Led by the beautiful painter Isis Lynch, the trio revolutionized the art world. Then suddenly, without explanation, Pussy Transmission vanished into historical obscurity. Now, twenty years later, three women come to Lynch Place. Lily and Nina are journalists desperate to interview Isis Lynch. Raven, on the other hand, wants to find her boyfriend, who's gone missing inside Isis's house. Raven's worried—she's heard that Pussy Transmission broke up because Isis began dabbling in black magic . . . with devastating results. All three women will shortly wish they'd never left home. Particularly once the rats in Lynch Place start warning them that they're going to die . . . and Raven meets Betty Butcher, the bouncy supernatural psycho who's intent on chopping her into bits. Pussy Transmission, Baby! Just because . . .

Burning Bulb
PUBLISHING

WOL-VRIEY
BIZARRO AND TRANSGRESSIVE FICTION

GIRLS ARE NOT SMILING

Welcome To The Road Trip From Hell

Pagan is demon-possessed.

Lori is suicidal.

Britt is just terminally pissed off.

Meet three young Boston women on the run from the law, each with problems that will fuse into more than the sum of their individual parts, becoming a holocaust of sex and violence and terror, a literal rain of blood and horror and gore and evil.

And if that wasn't already bad enough, Pagan's pet demon is slowly transforming her into something both unspeakable and unholy. Truly, these girls aren't smiling.

BLUE NIGHTMARES

Consummate EVIL is coming. It is relentless and unavoidable. It is Blue.

Jessica Schreiber is seeing things. Very horrible things. Since arriving in Raynham for what should have been a relaxing vacation, she's been seeing *The Big Blue*.

Jessica is smelling things too—dead and rotting things that she can't see. She is sure those dead and rotting things are dead people. Lots of dead people.

Jessica's worst nightmares will soon become her reality. Her reality will soon become a terrifying nightmare.

The tentacled residents of the House of Death have a lot that they wish to show Jessica Schreiber. They have a lot that they wish to tell her. But will she survive long enough to learn their lessons?

Burning Bulb
PUBLISHING

WOL-VRIEY
BIZARRO AND TRANSGRESSIVE FICTION

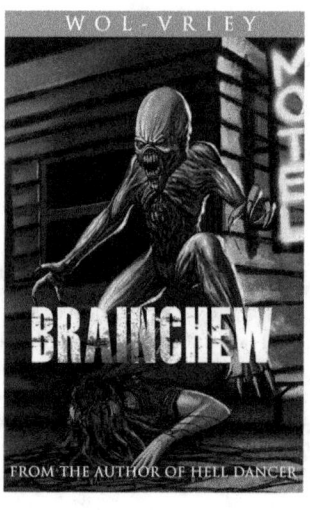

BRAINCHEW

It was supposed to be a simple jewel heist, but it went badly wrong. Chuck got shot and died.

Lance hid his friend's corpse in the Pleasant Street Cemetery. But that was a big mistake—there was something undead, something extremely hungry . . . something eXXXtremely horrible, buried in the Pleasant Street Cemetery.

And Lance had just woken it up.

They called the monster Brainchew because it ate brains. Human brains. And it preferred those brains fresh from the heads . . . of the living.

And now it was awake again, Brainchew planned on feeding big-time tonight. Oh hell yes, it did.

BRAINCHEW 2: OUT OF THEIR HEADS

After Tiff Hooper recognizes Josh Penham, the man who abducted her and kept her in his basement and abused her, she brings her three friends to Raynham for a night of well-deserved revenge on him.

Only things don't go according to plan.

It is never a good idea to leave a corpse in Raynham's Pleasant Street Cemetery. You run the very real risk of awakening what lies underground there. And that thing—Brainchew—is more horrible and more evil than anything the average mind conceives of even in its worst nightmares.

Brainchew is back! And this time the monster is extra-hungry. But there are plenty of delicious human brains about tonight, and Brainchew intends to eat them all before dawn.

Burning Bulb
PUBLISHING

WOL-VRIEY
BIZARRO AND TRANSGRESSIVE FICTION

DARIA: AN EROTIC NIGHTMARE

Even the best laid women can go wrong.

Daria Simpson is HUNGRY. She's HUNGRY for sex and bloodshed and death.

Shelly Parker just wanted to have a threesome with her boyfriend Craig and her best friend Erica. Everything was shaping up nicely for their weekend of sexual fun and games, until they stopped at the creepy Crossway Diner and met Daria.

From the moment they met Daria, EVERYTHING went wrong for them; and it went wrong in the most horrific and terrifying of ways!

Daria: Paranormal service has been resumed.

WET BONES

Greg is about learning the hard way that you don't mess with Aunt Grace.

Nine completely fleshless skeletons recovered in the Massachusetts woods. Two detectives on the trail of a horrible, hungry monster.

Broken-hearted Allie Jackson has a date with a creature from Hell.

Things are about to get well out of hand for everyone, and in horrifying, terrifying ways they don't expect.

Burning Bulb
PUBLISHING

WOL-VRIEY
BIZARRO AND TRANSGRESSIVE FICTION

MR. UGLY

When a rotting corpse appears and starts butchering Raynham's youths, there's really only one question that needs answering:

Is this faceless and rotting monster Peter Howard, or isn't it?

Problem is, Peter Howard died 15 years ago. So how can he possibly be back from the dead and murdering people with such relentless and incredible brutality?

Peter's mother Malicia, who's just been released from the lunatic asylum may have the answers to the crazy puzzle, but the two detectives investigating the deaths don't even know the right questions to ask her yet.

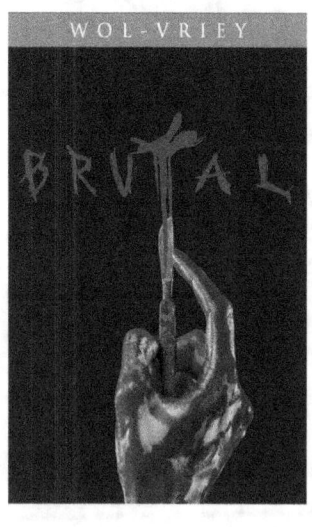

BRUTAL

Jane Winters is 28 years old.

She works as a checkout cashier in a department store. She's an attractive woman with a winning personality. She has both a photographic memory and an I.Q. of 189.

She's met the man of her dreams.

But she's also a cannibal with a unique and very scary mode of operation.

The group known as TULIP (The Urban Legend Investigation People) are out to either prove or disprove the legend of Insane Jane.

But have TULIP bitten off more than they can chew?

Burning Bulb
PUBLISHING

WOL-VRIEY
BIZARRO AND TRANSGRESSIVE FICTION

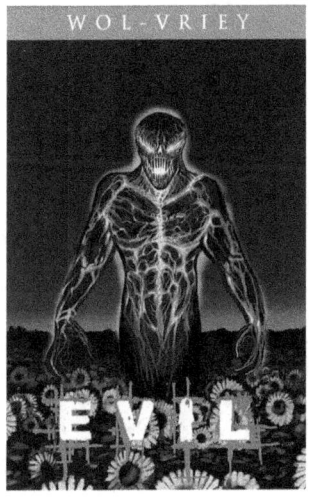

EVIL

The Evil began the week before Sylvia Stewart's 30th birthday.

Cathy Higgins died.

The Bargainer resurrected Cathy . . . for a price.

The price? Cathy's father Ronan had to plant some seeds for him.

But these were no ordinary seeds the Bargainer gave to Ronan Higgins. These were seeds from Hell: seeds which required human flesh as both soil and fertilizer.

And meanwhile, the unsuspecting Sylvia Stewart went ahead with the plans for her birthday party, which was to be held on Ronan Higgins' sunflower farm . . .

666

Ohio's State Route 666 stretches 14.7 miles between Zanesville and Dresden.

Most days, it's just a normal road with a funny name.

But for six minutes on the 6th of June each year, Route 666 becomes a gateway to somewhere else . . . a gateway to Hell.

Each year 13 unfortunates get trapped in the 666 underworld, with no way to get back home.

This year though, things are going to be very different. For one thing, there are currently a whole lot of turbulent human emotions at play in the underworld. And also . . . the psycho Al Gore is just about completing his collection of human heads.

And . . . what the hell is a church doing in Hell, of all places?

Burning Bulb
PUBLISHING

WOL-VRIEY
BIZARRO AND TRANSGRESSIVE FICTION

THE CLEAVERMAN

It began as a joke, a gag to pass the time that turned deadly. One rainy August night in Raynham, MA, nine friends jokingly invoke the evil phantom butcher called the Cleaverman.

These nine friends get a whole lot more than they ever bargained for. Because there's only one way to return the deadly Cleaverman back to the darkness he came from, and that is to solve his riddle, which starts: "Tell me the name of John Cleaverman's wife . . ."

And human beings being what we are, even with the Cleaverman out to butcher them all, our nine friends still manage to stir A WHOLE LOT of human misbehavior into the deadly mix.

At the rate they're going, it'll be a wonder if anyone survives THE CLEAVERMAN at all.

PERVERSE

When 21-year-old Heather Forrest accompanies three of her friends on a weekend trip up to Vermont, she has no idea what she's getting into.

Because, during a brief stop in the western Massachusetts woods, the girls get kidnapped and things go rapidly downhill from there. Soon Heather and her friends are fighting for their lives, fighting to survive the most perverted and impossible situation imaginable. And meanwhile, Hank Rollins is also in the woods, hunting the unholy monster that killed his wife and son . . . and he's hunting it with live human bait.

Oh yes, there will be blood. And there will be terror and buckets of gore also. And truly horrible atrocities will happen. Most definitely so.

Burning Bulb
PUBLISHING

www.ingramcontent.com/pod-product-compliance
Lightning Source LLC
Chambersburg PA
CBHW070020260626
47159CB00005B/1884